The
SECRETS
that we
KEEP

Copyright 2023 by Chrystal Miller

All rights reserved.
No portion of this book may be reproduced in any form without written permission from the publisher or author, except as permitted by U.S. copyright law.

Cover by N.Owens

This book is dedicated
to
anyone who had
a dream and dared
to follow it.

CONTENTS

CHAPTER 1
CHAPTER 2
CHAPTER 3
CHAPTER 4
CHAPTER 5
CHAPTER 6
CHAPTER 7
CHAPTER 8
CHAPTER 9
CHAPTER 10
CHAPTER 11
CHAPTER 12
CHAPTER 13
CHAPTER 14
CHAPTER 15
CHAPTER 16
CHAPTER 17
CHAPTER 18
CHAPTER 19
CHAPTER 20
CHAPTER 21
CHAPTER 22
CHAPTER 23
CHAPTER 24
CHAPTER 25
CHAPTER 26
ABOUT THE AUTHOR
ALSO BY

Chapter 1

Rhyann

I look at my watch. It's a quarter to four, almost time to go home. If only this god forsaken meeting would end. I sit behind my boss as he conducts the Board of Directors' meeting for Devereux Publications. As the CEO of my grandfather's company, he makes the executive decisions.

Until my twenty-fifth birthday, that is. For now, I've spent every summer working as his assistant, taking notes during meetings, fetching his coffee every morning, and making sure his lunch appointments aren't missed. I prepare the information on whatever important call he has with clients. I basically do all the grunt work for him, for free.

Sure, I have the trust funds from both of my parents. But the idea of working for free sours me a little. Especially when I'm working for Adrian Crawford, my dead father's best friend. A man so cold-hearted, he refused to hire his own son.

He and my father had been best friends since early childhood. They grew up together, running in the same social circles, and even went to the same college. That was where my father met my mother, Adrian met his wife Lenora, and the four of them made grandiose plans for their futures. Together.

Thirty years later, after the deaths of both my parents, then my grandfather, and Adrian's wife running off with some tattooed biker she met while sneaking out to dive bars on the outskirts of the city, here I am. The last member of the Devereux family, heiress to a Fortune 500 company, and personal assistant to the man running my family's company.

"I think that's it. Enjoy your long weekend. I'll see some of you tonight at the charity auction?" Adrian says cheerily to his team before standing. I blink my eyes, focusing on the rigid back of the man sitting at the head of the conference table.

Adrian turns and looks at me. "Miss Devereux, you're dismissed for the evening. Enjoy your long weekend." I nod my head quietly and turn to leave. "Oh, and Rhyann, congratulations," he adds softly.

I smile, my cheeks heating to a light blush. Looking down at my feet, I walk out of the conference room. Yesterday, I graduated from college. At twenty-four years old. In nine months, when I turn twenty-five, I'll be able to take over my grandfather's company.

The small flame of pride is quickly snuffed out by the lurch of missing my parents. They would have been proud to see me graduate with my MBA, just like my dad and grandfather.

I hadn't expected to see anyone sitting in the crowd to support me yesterday, but Adrian was there. He sat proudly, watching the ceremony like all the parents in the crowd. It was kind of him, and I appreciate the support he's given since my grandfather died four years ago, but it isn't the same. Having a doting grandfather and a pseudo uncle in your corner feels different than having two loving parents around to support you.

Not that I would know what having that is like, either. My mom died when I was nine. My dad, well, he took his own life a year later. He couldn't stand the idea of living a life without his Sophia. He didn't have the strength to go on without her, not even for his own daughter.

Papa and Adrian, and for a short time Lenora, were there to help me through the hardest parts of losing both parents. Lenora still sends me letters from time to time—even though I tell her in every letter she can just text me or DM me on any of my socials. I think she's the only person in the world who uses the good old USPS instead of emailing or sending a text. She even sent a bouquet of roses to the office today to congratulate me on my degree.

Devereux Publications isn't far from my apartment. With the time being close to eight o'clock, I decide to take an Uber home rather than walk with a bunch of flowers. The walk isn't far, but I just feel like the safer and more responsible thing is to get a ride.

My apartment is on the southwestern side of the city and overlooks the ocean. The building is one of the many owned by Devereux Publications, owned by me. I brace myself against the doorframe of my front door. The very thought of everything I own, or will own in nine months, makes my head spin. It's all so overwhelming.

Papa made sure I never needed or wanted anything growing up, but he also made sure I was humble and thankful for everything I had. So much so that, when he sent me off to Evangeline's at thirteen years old, all the other well-to-do girls thought I was a scholarship kid, not an entitled heiress to a rich corporation.

THE SECRETS THAT WE KEEP   5

Scholarship girls at Evangeline's, an all-girls private school, were nothing more than tools for the future socialites to use in perfecting their social savagery and manipulation of those they deemed beneath them. For the first year, that was me. A social cockroach. That's what the upper-class girls called all the scholarship girls. They believed anyone there on a scholarship was a bottom feeder, a pest who fed off the droppings and leftovers of the elite.

Then Papa showed up on Family Day that first year and the reigning queen bee discovered that I had more money, more connections, more social influence than she ever would. Which made her and her little hive even more vicious and vindictive.

But I pushed through with my head held high. I made it through six years at the school and was the only one in my class to get into Hartley, my parents' alma mater.

With a sigh, I leave the beautiful flowers on the marble table in the entryway. It's dark and eerily quiet. *I should get a cat*, I think to myself. *Or maybe a dog*. I wouldn't say I'm a lonely person; I have friends, but they're all off living their best lives before they settle down in their respective careers. I've never been great at social functions or large crowds, always afraid I'd say the wrong thing, so I keep my circle small.

Adrian is always telling me I need to work on my social skills if I'm to take over the company soon. I suck the inside of my cheek between my teeth, thinking about having to deal with all that. The social circles I'm going to have to navigate, the elbows I'll have to rub, and the people I will have to pretend to like. It all makes me nauseous.

My body lurches forward and I'm struggling to breathe. I blink my eyes, trying to push past the darkness of sleep. What the hell? The joints in my shoulders burn as I try to lift my hands to my face. It's now that I feel the sticky pull of whatever is holding my wrists together behind my back. The same tacky feeling binds my ankles together, too.

The salty, acrid smell of sweat and booze assaults my nostrils. The scent is putrid and sours whatever is left in my stomach. I fight the heaving sensation that's taking over me. My heart races as my mind scrambles to figure out what's going on. I feel like I'm going to puke, but my mouth is bound shut too, and I'm trying not to cry.

Strong arms hold my body tight against whoever's carrying me. Where they're carrying me to, I can't tell. I don't even know how long I've been like this, bound and gagged by duct tape. I'm blindfolded, the fabric tied so tightly around my head that it's difficult to open my eyes. Not that it would matter. I doubt I'd be able to see, anyway.

I fight against the tape binding me. My muffled screams barely make it past my lips as I squirm and push with all the energy I can muster. It's no use though. The strong arms holding me readjust to deal with my moving body.

With a swirling dizziness that feels like I'm being flung into the air by a bungee cord, my chest hits the soft wall of my captors' back. All the blood rushes to my head, my hips bent over what I can only assume is the person's shoulders. My nostrils, my only mode of breathing at the moment, fill with the rancid smell of swamp ass. I can't fight the lurching my stomach does this time. All I can do is swallow back the bitter wine-tinged bile that rises from my throat and fills my mouth.

I'd happily welcome back the sweaty booze smell over this person's shit stained swamp ass stench. Trails of moisture run down my eyelids and over my forehead, getting caught in my mess of hair. I can't tell if the tears are from anger and fear of what's happening to me, or if it's from the continuous heaving of my stomach.

I'm being kidnapped. Holy shit! I'm actually being kidnapped. Realization hits harder than a diesel truck slamming against a brick wall, and I fight my captor more as blood continues to rush to my head.

I can't smell anything past the cocktail of putrid body odor, but from the muffled sounds around me and the cool air hitting my bare legs, we aren't in my apartment anymore. We're somewhere outside on the street.

We stop moving, and meaty fingertips grip my hips to thrust my body up and over their shoulders. My head flings back and I'm dropped onto a hard, carpeted surface.. Judging from the smell of motor oil, I've just been dumped in the trunk of a car. It's a welcome reprieve, though, from the horrendous smells coming off the body of whoever carried me down here.

My body struggles fruitlessly against the bindings as the abrasive carpeting scratches my bare skin. My kidnapper is going to close the trunk any minute now, and even though I can't see anything, I know I need to find my way out before it's too late.

THE SECRETS THAT WE KEEP   9

Only, nothing moves, the vehicle doesn't shift, and there's no sound of a trunk closing. All I hear is the rustling of movement in the distance, along with some very aggressive grunting.

"Motherfucker," a familiar voice growls somewhere nearby.

Within seconds, warm, firm hands are scooping me up from where I was dumped, and I'm gently placed upright on what feels like concrete. The blindfold is slowly pulled from my eyes, a random strand of hair tangled and tugging in the fabric.

"The police are on their way," that same familiar voice informs me as I blink away the darkness and my eyes begin to focus on who my savior could be.

Chapter 2

Rhyann

"What do you mean, you can't find him?" Adrian yells at the uniformed officer inside my apartment. "You have the piece of shit Buick that the bastard was going to lock her in."

He looks over at me, his face red with fury, his salt and pepper hair a disheveled mess. It's a stark contrast to the tuxedo he wears. He was at one of the many charity balls Devereux Publications hosts every year when he got the call from the police.

"You okay?" a soft, deep voice asks, breaking me from the shock of what just happened.

I turn to look into the silver eyes of Tate Crawford, my oldest friend and Adrian's only son. He smiles at me, sliding a glass of amber liquid in my direction.

The sweet, spicy notes of berries and citrus hit my tongue as I down the offered glass of whiskey. "Thanks," I manage to choke out.

"You know, that's a thirteen hundred dollar vintage scotch, and you just downed it like it was a shot of Jim Beam," Tate chuckles.

"What the fuck, Tate?" I sputter.

"Doesn't matter. I'm just fucking glad you're okay." Tate and I have always had a complicated friendship. Enemy-ship? Frenemies? I honestly can't explain the relationship we have. Just that we have one. "I'd hate to know what would have happened if I didn't show up when I did."

Me too, I think to myself. I just nod in agreement, still trying to process everything that happened.

When Tate pulled the blindfold from my eyes, I couldn't figure out where I was. All I knew was that I was outside, sitting on a curb, facing the tire of an old, beat up, black Buick Century. The trunk was open, and just as I had thought, my mouth, wrists and ankles were covered in duct tape.

I couldn't form the words in my head to speak when the police arrived. Adrian is hot on their heels, so he's been doing most of the talking, or yelling, really. Apparently, Tate had been coming up to the apartment when he saw a man come around the corner with me flung over his shoulder.

Tate didn't know it was me until he made a move to intervene in the attempted abduction. I wonder if that little bit of knowledge would have stopped him from saving me, but I don't bring it up. Not in front of his father, or the police.

Tate and I have gone back and forth for years. A long, delicate dance between being friends and hating one another with more passion than the daytime soaps his mother loved to watch when we were kids.

"Miss Devereux, can you tell us anything that might help us find the person who broke into your apartment?" an officer asks. She's one of the four uniformed officers currently milling about my apartment, examining every minute detail of my life.

"No, I told you. I woke up blindfolded and duct taped." I slide the empty whiskey glass back to Tate, silently asking for a refill. "The first thing I saw was Tate, when he pulled the blindfold off my face."

Tate winks at me, his silver-gray eyes sparkling in the bright light of my kitchenette.

THE SECRETS THAT WE KEEP   13

"Is it possible that Mister Crawford had something to do with this?" Her voice is low as she nods her head in Tate's direction.

"Tate does not smell like rotten swamp ass and booze," I tell the officer with a laugh.

"Awe, I love you too, Boo," Tate says sarcastically.

I roll my eyes, taking the glass from his outstretched hand. With a smirk, I tack on, "Well, not today, at least."

The officer lets out a frustrated sigh. "Okay, Miss Devereux. So, you came home from work, changed your clothes, and sat down with a glass of wine."

"Yes," I tell her for the millionth time in the past hour. "I had two glasses in bed and fell asleep reading."

My heart rate picks up recalling how I woke to a total loss of senses and being moved around by someone whose face I never saw. "All I remember is the smell. He stunk, like he hadn't showered in weeks." I shudder.

Tears sting my eyes, and Tate nods his head at the glass in my hand, not once taking his eyes off me. I notice purple and blue forming over the swollen pink flesh around one of his eyes.

I pieced together most of what happened from his interview with the police. He said he was coming to see me. He wanted to congratulate me on finishing college when he saw the kidnapping. He went to stop it, always trying to be everyone's hero—everyone but mine—and that was when he realized it was me in the trunk. He fought with the kidnapper, and as the guy ran away, Tate called the police, who called Adrian, and here we are now.

"I think she's told you enough, officers." Adrian comes over to where Tate, the female officer, and I are talking. If you can call it talking. She's asking questions, questions she has asked me several times in the past hour, and I've given the same answer each time.

Tate is just standing there doing what Tate does best, wooing people with his radiant smile and beautiful eyes. He makes me want to throw this over priced whiskey in his gorgeous face.

"Just one more question, Mister Crawford, then we will be done." She looks from Adrian back to me. "When was the last time you spoke to your father?"

What? I choke on the liquor I have been sipping—now that I know it's expensive as fuck. "You're joking, right?" I ask, looking from the officer, to Adrian, then to Tate for help comprehending her question.

The officer writes my response on the small notepad she'd been taking notes on since she got here. "We'll be in touch, Miss Devereux. Mister Crawford, a word outside, please?"

Adrian follows all four officers out of my apartment, and I let out a deep breath I hadn't realized I was holding in. I lift the glass to my lips and down the last bit of the expensive whiskey, not even caring about the price tag at this point.

"Hey, you okay?" Tate's warm hand touches my cheek, catching the silent tears rolling down my cheek.

I don't know why I'm crying. Maybe it's the weight of everything lifting, the severity of what could have happened to me finally setting in. Or is it the mention of my father? The man who was too weak, too cowardly to face the world without my mother.

"Yeah." I clear my throat, swiping at those renegade tears. "I'm fine. What were you doing here this late, anyway?"

Tate laughs. It's a soft, light laugh, not mocking, but caring. Like he's trying to lighten my mood. "Rhy, it's barely ten o'clock."

Huh? No. I suck in a breath, processing those four words. Barely ten o'clock. "That's impossible," I tell him as the blood drains from my face.

"How so?" he asks sincerely, concern written all over his face.

"I got home shortly after eight. There's no way I've been home for two hours," I explain when he looks at me, concern morphing into confusion.

"How much wine did you drink?" Tate's voice is sharp, not at all the gentle caress it was five minutes ago.

"I don't know, two. No more than two glasses. The bottle should still be in my room."

Without another word, Tate takes off down the hall to my bedroom, the only bedroom in the apartment. He comes right back out, a half a bottle of wine and a nearly full glass in his hands. He doesn't even look at me; he heads straight for the door where his father and the police officers are still talking.

After a few seconds of raised voices and muffled words, Tate comes back in and holds his hand out to me.

"Let's go."

I look up in confusion. My brain still hasn't fully cleared away the fog left behind from being woken from a deep sleep. "Umm, where are we going?" I ask hesitantly.

"To the hospital. Come on. Dad's having Maisie come by to pack your bags for you."

"Why?" I give him a skeptical look. Now that the panic has settled, my brain feels muddled, fuzzy, almost like I'm still drunk from the night before.

Only, it's still the night before, and aside from two shots of expensive whiskey, I have had little to drink. I sigh and take Tate's hand. He gives my fingers a gentle squeeze and pulls me close against his chest.

I can feel his heart racing as he presses his lips to the top of my head and says, "I'll explain everything on the way to the hospital. But you're not coming back to this apartment, Rhyann."

I ride with Tate to the hospital. There's an awkward silence in the car as we speed through traffic lights. The hum of the engine echoes through my mind.

Would I have been able to hear the engine in that trunk? What about the smell of gasoline? Would I smell the gas and oil coursing through the various pipes and hoses under the car like the blood coursing through my veins? Not that I can smell my blood. Not while it's still inside me.

Would he have killed me? My attacker, what was his plan with me? I'm nobody special, no one significant. Not yet, at least.

"Well, so much for congratulations," Tate grimaced, painting a fake smile across his face.

"What?" I ask, pulling myself from the haze of my own thoughts.

"My dad," Tate goes on. It's obvious the small talk is as much for me as it is for him. "He told me you were in town and where you were staying."

"Oh," I laugh awkwardly. "Yeah."

Suddenly, Tate stops the car and looks at me. My chest starts heaving as my breathing picks up. I turn from looking at Tate to the windshield. The traffic light is red.

"Why didn't you go home to your grandfather's place? Kathleen would have had everything ready for you. You don't need to live in the apartment anymore now that you're done with school."

Kathleen is—or was—my grandfather's personal assistant. She manages the day-to-day duties and maintenance of the inside of the house, while her husband, Phil, maintains the grounds.

After my grandfather died, Adrian and I both agreed to keep the couple on to continue to manage the property while I was in college and had no need for the place. Even out of school, I feel intimidated by the sprawling, gated estate. Kathleen and Phil are family to me, though, just as Adrian and Tate are.

"You think someone tried to drug me, don't you?" My words come out softly; my voice sounds so childlike and fragile.

I can't help the naivety in my question. This entire ordeal, I've been talked about, talked down to, and even just left completely out. No one wants to actually explain to me what happened and what's going on.

"I think so," is all he says, his words sharp and to the point. "But you didn't answer my question, Rhyann."

I look anywhere I can, except at Tate. How can I explain just how empty that house feels? How it's not my home, hasn't been for a very long time. Not since I went away to boarding school.

We don't say another word the rest of the way to the hospital. Once we arrive, Take pulls his Phantom Black Audi TTS right up to the doors.

In true privileged fashion, a gaggle of nurses waits at the door with a wheelchair, like I'm some expectant mother coming in to have a baby.

"I'll be in as soon as I park," Tate assures me as he opens my door and helps me into the waiting chair.

"What, no valet?" I ask with an eye roll. The whole *having more money than I know what to do with* thing unnerves me.

My papa made sure I knew the value of a dollar and understood that a person's character should not be measured by the numbers in their bank account.

Reluctantly, I settle into the wheelchair and allow myself to be led to a private exam room on one of the higher floors, away from the everyday denizens waiting to be seen in the emergency room. Just another perk to frivolous wealth and privilege.

The nurses set out a backless gown and leave the room, expecting me to change, like I'm going to allow them to admit me and stay for a spell. Um, no. I toss the gown on the small chair in the corner and wait at the edge of the bed for the nurse to return.

The woman comes in and stops abruptly when she sees that I'm still in the shorts and oversized t-shirt I came in wearing.

"Oh, honey. You're supposed to put the gown on," she says as she sets the blood draw kit down on the metal table next to the bed. "Here, let me help you."

"No. That's unnecessary. I'm not staying," I explain, holding my arms out, giving her access to my veins. "Just take my blood, an Uber is already on its way."

"Oh, but the police and Mister Crawford wanted a rape kit done as well."

I don't fight the involuntary lurch I make. "I can assure you, if I'd been raped, I would know. Now, can you just draw the blood so I can get out of here before *Mister* Crawford comes back?"

"I'm sorry. I just can't. I was given specific instructions: draw your blood and wait for the doctor to come in and examine you," the nurse confesses in a commanding voice, almost like she is the one with all the control in this room.

Well, she has a thing or two to learn. Someone almost took my control from me once tonight, and I'm not about to let some woman with a god complex who thinks she has the authority to decide for me tell me what I need.

"Then I'm leaving," I say, my mind finally clear of the drug-induced fog.

"You can't do that," she calls as I push my way past her and out of the private exam room.

Her voice carries down the hall as she calls for security. They can't force me to stay for some stupid ass blood work, and if the police really need it for whatever waste of time investigation they plan to do, they can have their happy asses in here with me.

I just want to go home. I don't want to be at the hospital. I don't want some doctor doing an exam that I really feel I don't need, and I definitely don't want to have anyone make choices for me that I can make for myself. And I choose to go home.

The elevator dings open and I step inside, the nurse from my room catching my eye as the doors begin to slide closed. She's at the nurses' station, on the phone with someone, staring daggers in my direction. I can't help the laugh that escapes my throat as I wave goodbye.

I look at my phone on the way down. The Uber app says my driver has just arrived at the emergency room entrance. Suddenly, the thought that my driver could be my would-be kidnapper pops into my head. A sick sort of panic rises from my stomach and blooms in my chest. My heart is racing, and I'm finding it hard to breathe.

Fuck, what am I doing? Someone almost kidnapped me tonight. Where are the police? Why aren't they here? Why were they spending so much time talking to Adrian and not me? Or even Tate. Tate saw the kidnapper, he saved me for Christ's sake. I've never felt as alone as I do right now in this elevator. The brushed metal walls and sterile tile floor feel like they're closing in on me, slowly crushing me with the weight of what happened this evening.

My back hits the cool metal walls, and I slide down until my barely covered ass hits the ground. I hug my knees to my chest and let down the dam that's been holding my feelings back.

I feel the elevator come to a stop and have just enough time to pull myself from my impending panic attack before the doors slide open. And my god am I glad that I am standing because the crowd of people at the elevator doors when they open is enough to frighten even the most hardened criminal.

Adrian and Tate are standing there with murderous intent written all over their faces. Behind them is the female officer from my apartment, a man I assume to be her partner because he's the only other uniformed officer there, and two unfamiliar faces. Both men, both wearing suits that look like they were taken off and left on the floor, only to be quickly thrown back on to come down here.

Fuck me. I groan when I see them, and try my best to push my way past the crowd. I get as far as the two men in cheap suits before strong, warm fingers wrap around my arm.

"Rhyann. What's wrong?" Tate asks, pushing through the small crowd of people.

"Nothing, I just want to go home." I will not cry in front of him, or Adrian.

"Then I'll take you." Tate wraps his arm around my waist.

"Son, we need to know if she was drugged," Adrian speaks up. "Rhyann, I'm so sorry, sweetheart. I'm just worried about you."

Tate looks at one of the crumpled suits. "If you test the wine, can you tell if there were any kind of drugs in it?" he asks.

"Well, yes." The man's voice is nasally and grates on my nerves.

"Good. Rhy, let's go." Tate pushes past the throng of testosterone. Yes, even the female officer is oozing with testosterone at the moment. If you've never seen a woman who has bigger balls than a lot of men, you haven't met a successful woman who's killing it in a "man's job".

"However," the other wrinkled suit guy speaks up, "if we draw her blood, we could determine how much she ingested."

"Do you want to stay?" Tate asks me, which obviously irritates the officers. His father just stands there silently, a small smile ticking at the corners of his mouth.

I shake my head no. The last thing I want to do is see that same nurse gloat over me being escorted back to that room by four police officers.

"Send a traveling nurse to her grandfather's house," Tate commands, and we leave the waiting room without another word.

Chapter 3

Rhyann

Adrian isn't far behind us as we leave the hospital. The drive to my grandfather's house isn't long, and we're relatively silent.

I don't have any clothes other than the pajamas I'm wearing and the pair of vans I slipped on before leaving the house.

"I'm not going to ask if you're okay. I know you're not." Tate breaks the unrelenting silence as we step through the door from the mudroom into the kitchen.

I half expected to find a layer of dust on every surface in the house, but I already know Kathleen cleans the house daily. Since no one has lived here in two years, she cleans a different room each day. I can't help but wonder if the bedrooms are as immaculate as the kitchen.

I look at the large Sub-Zero fridge with front panels that match the ornate cabinetry of the rest of the kitchen.

THE SECRETS THAT WE KEEP   27

My stomach chooses now to growl in response to Tate's love of stating the obvious.

"I'm fine," I tell him.

"Liar," Tate laughs. "I've already texted Devon. He's bringing pizza and beer."

I groan. Devon Morris, Tate's best friend. He was also my first kiss, the one who took my virginity, and the first person to ever lie to me and break my heart. He's the very last person I want to see right now.

"Yeah, and I'm off to bed. It's been a long night." I wave in Tate's direction and push the door to the hall open.

"Hold on, Rhyann," Adrian says gently from behind me.

I turn slowly to face my boss, my father's best friend, and the closest thing to family I've had in the past two years. I don't want to hurt his feelings, but I am really not in the mood to drag any of this bullshit on tonight. "Adrian, please," I sigh.

"I know you're tired and hungry, Rhyann. Let's talk about what happened and then, after the boys come with pizza, you can go to bed." He pats one of the lacquered oak bar stools tucked under the lip of the counter.

I groan, my shoulders slumping forward as I drag my feet over to the stool. I know this isn't mature behavior for someone who is less than a year away from taking over her family business. Why act like an adult when the men in your life don't treat you like one? Well, man in your life.

Does Tate really count? I have only seen him on holidays and the occasional night of bar hopping during summer breaks, when I would get roped into being the designated driver for the other assistants at the office. He always had some barely dressed blonde with giant tits on his arm, sometimes two. Devon and his brother Liam were always right there behind him.

Devon is never afraid to make a bad joke at my expense. *Red on the head like the noodle of a poodle*, the brothers would say to me. As we got older, the jokes and the jabs changed. A lot changed as we got older. For one, I went away to boarding school when I was thirteen and the boys fifteen. Every summer I came home, but things were different between all of us until the last summer before college. The summer when it was just me and Devon.

"Adrian, can't this wait until tomorrow? Please?" I plead, plopping down onto the hard seat.

"I'm sorry, kiddo. But the best time to get everything out is when it's fresh on the mind," he says in a comforting, fatherly tone.

"But is it really fresh on the mind? It's after eleven. All this happened a couple hours ago," Tate questions. *Thank you Tate*, I think to myself.

"She's finally clear minded and, Rhyann, I know what happened tonight is running through your mind on repeat." Adrian smirks at me, an all-knowing look in his silver eyes. The same silver as his son's.

"There's not much to say. I mean, I was almost kidnapped." I turn my gaze to Tate. "Until he showed up and saved me."

"Not all heroes wear capes," Tate gives me a wink and a smile. "But seriously, Rhy. What happened before that?"

I suck the side of my cheek between my teeth and think. "Nothing," I say blandly. "I came home, thought about getting a cat, changed out of my work clothes, and settled down with a glass of wine. The next thing I knew, I was flung over someone's shoulder. I couldn't see, I couldn't move; all I could do was smell him, and he smelled like shit."

"Who smells like shit?" Devon's voice cuts through the tension in the room. I look up to see him pushing through the door with a stack of pizzas in his hands, Liam right behind him carrying two cases of Sierra Nevada Flipside.

"Your mom," I say, not skipping a beat. "Anyway, that's everything. Can I go now Adrian?"

"Awe. What did the little demon do to get into trouble this time?" Liam asks.

"Go ahead. But Rhyann, please eat something before you go to bed," Adrian sighs and turns to face his son's two best friends. "Boys. Tate, I assume you and Dummy One and Dummy Two are going to stay here tonight."

"Yes, sir." I hear Tate say as I'm walking out of the kitchen.

My old bedroom is as dust free as the kitchen, and the linens are all fresh. Kathleen is a powerhouse. The woman deserves a raise for how well she maintains this ostentatious show of wealth my grandfather called an estate. I run a bath in my private ensuite bathroom, delighted that Kathleen has even kept my favorite soaps and shampoos stocked on the off chance that I'd come home. *Surprise!* I'm home, Kathleen, and your attention to detail has paid off.

I know Adrian asked me to eat something, but I just can't stomach being around Tate, Liam, and Devon tonight, not after everything that happened—or almost happened.

I'm not sure how long I sit in the tub, but the water has turned tepid by the time there's a soft knock on the bathroom door.

"Rhyann," a low male voice calls from the other side. "Hey, I brought you a couple slices of pizza."

I groan and slide my body down the surface of the tub. I'm not sure how long I had passed out earlier, but it was long enough for my would-be kidnapper to gag me and tie me up with duct tape. I'm sure I can hold my breath and stay under water long enough for the man on the other side of the door to get the hint and go away.

After a couple minutes, I push up out of the water with a splash, gasping for air.

"Rhy, I was joking about the demon part," Liam calls. Well, there goes my plan to wait him out. "I'm sorry."

He sounds strangely desperate. I mean, we do have history. History I know he would never tell his brother about. Even though Dev and I also have history, Dev would tell Tate, and then I'd hate to see what Tate would do to Liam. They might be best friends, but Tate drew a line in the sand a long time ago. I was on one side, the boys on the other. It was a line none of us admitted to crossing, but the brothers and I had.

"Liam, it's fine. Thank you for the pizza," I sigh and push my wet hair back from my face. "Leave it on the bedside table for me, please. I'll be out soon."

I don't hear anything else from the other side of the door as I stand from the tub and dry myself off. Slipping into the soft, purple terry-cloth robe that I found hanging from a hook on the door, I step into my childhood bedroom.

I look down at the pile of clothes at the foot of the bed. I forgot I don't have any clothes here, and I don't want to wear the same clothes I had on earlier, when I was almost kidnapped.

"Tate also asked us to bring you some clean clothes," Liam says from my closed bedroom door. He slides a small canvas backpack across the hardwood floor. "Don't worry, they're some of Gemma's old things."

"Uh, thanks?" I didn't mean for it to come out as a question, but what the fuck is he doing in my room? "Now, can you get out? I'd like to change, eat, and go to sleep, if you don't mind."

"I do, actually." Liam pushes off the door and walks slowly in my direction. I watch him watch me as he approaches, but my feet refuse to move. Either I'm just too tired to fight him, or something in my brain was damaged from whatever drugs were slipped into my wine earlier.

"Liam, don't be stupid. What are you going to do if Tate catches you in here?" I breathe out when he is right in front of me, his big wall of a chest taking up all my personal space.

"What should I do, Rhy?" He tips my chin up to meet his eyes. Eyes so blue it was like some ancient god captured the sky and put it in his gaze. I was hypnotized by that gaze once, and his mouth. I moan just thinking about his mouth and all the things Liam did to me with it.

"I'm not playing this game with you again, Liam," I warn him.

"Tate told us what happened." His tone is sad, apologetic. "Are you okay?"

Seriously? Why does everyone keep asking me that question? What little control I held onto suddenly snaps. "As a matter of fact, no. I'm not okay, Liam. I am not doing well at all." I seethe, pushing at his chest. "Someone drugged me. In my apartment. Then my wrists were duct taped, and so were my ankles and my mouth. A smelly fucking blindfold was tied so tightly over my eyes,

I couldn't have opened them if I wanted to. And I did want to."

The tears I'd been carefully keeping at bay fall from my lashes, but I keep going. "Before you ask if I saw him, or heard his voice, no. I didn't. I couldn't see or hear anything the entire time. But I could smell him." Bile rises in my throat at the memory of his putrid swamp ass and sweaty booze smell.

"Fucking hell, Rhyann," Liam says, wrapping his big arms around my small frame.

"He smelled like shit, Liam. Literal shit, rancid booze, and sweat." I cry into his chest.

I take a deep breath and inhale a scent that is all Liam. He smells like citrus and sage and being out in the woods at the back of Papa's property—my property now, I guess. His strong hands stroke up and down my spine, the mix of his scent and the strong comfort of his touch washing away all the nightmarish memories of my faceless kidnapper.

I don't know how long this peace between the two of us will last, but I'll take comfort while he's offering it, and I just cry. I let all the stress, the fear and the anger I've felt since Tate pulled me from the trunk of that old car, out in Liam's arms.

THE SECRETS THAT WE KEEP   35

"God, I've missed you Rhyann," Liam confesses.

I can't help the soft, sorrowful laugh that escapes me. I planned to call him in the morning, see if he wanted to meet up for coffee. We've had an on and off fling every summer since my grandfather died.

"Don't lie," I whisper into his chest. "I'm well aware of all the gorgeous women you've been with since the last time I saw you."

Our little arrangement has always been an open one as far as seeing other people. We both agreed to keep it from his brother, Tate, and Adrian. I've been to enough funerals already, I don't want to attend Liam's.

"What? Are you stalking my socials?" he laughs.

"Not at all." The banter helps the tears stop.

"Hey." He tips my chin up to look into his beautiful blue eyes. "I'm not going to let anything happen to you."

"Promises, promises," I laugh as his full, warm lips brush over mine. How we're going to manage whatever it is between us, and keep it a secret, is beyond me. Not if his brother and the Crawford men are hovering around like protective watchdogs.

Chapter 4

Rhyann

I didn't eat my pizza last night, and when I woke this morning, I realized I never put pajamas on. I'm still swaddled in the purple robe, but I'm also tucked safely in the big four-poster canopy bed in my childhood bedroom.

"Liam," I gasp, bolting upright. I quickly throw the duvet off me and look around for the bag of Gemma's clothes he brought me last night.

I find the backpack sitting nicely on top of the dresser at the back of my walk-in closet, which still has all the painfully embarrassing clothes mom would force me to wear when I was young.

Gemma was the third member of the Morris triplets. She looked nothing like her brothers. Where they were blonde haired and blue eyed, Gemma's hair was as black as night, and her eyes were so dark it was like looking into a bottomless well. But she was one of the nicest girls

THE SECRETS THAT WE KEEP   37

I'd ever known. I was fifteen when she was raped and murdered. The police said it was a couple of kids from the public school in town. Gemma had been dating one of her classmates, and when they did the rape kit post mortem, his DNA was an exact match for the semen left behind. I was supposed to come home and finish school in town until that happened.

Two years later, my grandfather retired early, after a mild heart attack at the office. He told me I had already lost two parents, so it would be cruel for fate to take him from me too. He wasn't wrong. There isn't a day that goes by where I don't miss him. Maybe that's why it's taken me two years to come back here, to the home my grandfather raised me in. Maybe that's why I'm not excited to take over the company in nine months.

I push the depressing thoughts aside and pull out the clothes one of the guys stuffed into the backpack. To be honest, I expected to find some outdated fashion choices from the early 2010s, but the choices they brought me were so basic, they could probably pass as something from any decade in the past half century. There's a pair of black leggings a little long for my legs. Gemma was taller than me by a good six inches. Her legs were long and slender, like a ballerina. I find a black tank top with a built-in bra inside the bag, too. Thankfully, even though this too is long on me, the chest part is a perfect fit. I don't find any panties inside the bag, which I'm a little thankful for. It's one thing to wear a dead woman's clothes, another to wear her panties.

I dress in the borrowed clothes, thankful that I don't have to walk around my grandfather's house in nothing but a robe, and I make my way to the kitchen.

When I get there, it's quiet. No one is around. No Tate, Liam, or Devon. I let out a sigh of relief. I know eventually I will have to face the three of them, and I'm sure Tate knows by now that I cried myself to sleep in Liam's arms. I just don't know if I can do it on an empty stomach.

Thankfully, there's still plenty of leftover pizza in the fridge when I open it. I look through the boxes until I find the one with the Hawaiian pizza. Hawaiian is the best when it's leftover and cold the next morning.

I don't bother getting a plate from the cabinet. Like a true college student, I improvise and just eat over the pizza box.

"Such a heathen. Don't you have any manners?" a male voice asks from the door to the mudroom.

"Fuck off, Devon," I say with a mouthful of pizza.

He chuckles and walks over, plopping down on the barstool next to me. "I was just teasing you, Red."

I turn my head to glare at the person next to me. Devon must be trying to push my buttons this morning. Why else would he call me by the nickname I hate the most? "How much did Adrian pay you to be nice?" I blurt out and immediately regret the cruel tone of my voice.

He gives me the biggest smile and throws his hands up in the air. "Hey. I'm just glad you're okay, Rhyann," he confesses in a low voice, a gravity in his tone I've only heard a handful of times.

"Thanks, Dev." I don't know what else to say to that. His eyes are downcast, and his perpetual scowl is turned down further in a frown.

The guys and I have been in each other's lives pretty much since diapers. They've always picked on me one way or another. But whenever I needed them, they were there. They helped me pick up the pieces of my shattered world, and helped me put it back together.

Me, Gemma, Tate, Liam, and Devon. We were a dream team. Then Gemma died, and the guys treated me differently. They held me at a distance. At times Devon was more cruel than the others. Liam always followed whatever his brother did, but when it was just the two of us, he was different, kinder to me.

"Oh good. She's alive," Liam says as he walks through the same door his twin had just come from.

"Read the room, dude." Devon snarls at his brother, then looks me over. I'm wearing his sister's clothes and he knows it. They both do. It can't be easy for them to see me sitting here, like this, after everything that happened last night.

"Whatever, man." Liam comes to stand next to me and looks at the pizza. "Disgusting. Now I know why Tate wanted a ham and pineapple pizza." Liam makes a mocking gag sound.

I give him my biggest smile before slowly lifting the slice in my hand to my mouth. My tongue darts out, pink tip touching the edge of the pizza crust, lapping up a stray drop of cold sauce. "Mmm," I moan. With a deliberately steady pace, I open my mouth as wide as I can, guiding the end of the cheesy piece in, resting the flaky, cold crust on the surface of my tongue, not once breaking eye contact with Liam.

A smile creeps across my face as my mouth closes, my teeth sinking into the congealed cheese. "Mmmm. So fucking good," I moan.

I wait for a reaction from Liam as I slowly chew the food in my mouth, but all he does is watch me with hooded eyes.

"Quit fucking with my brother's head, Rhyann," Devon warns me.

I turn to the other brother. Their features are nearly identical. Genetically speaking, they are identical twins. They split from the same fertilized egg, creating two identical but very different embryos. Their features are the same. Golden blonde hair that lightens in the summer and darkens in the winter, eyes the color of a summer sky. They both tower over me at a whopping six foot six inches tall, and both men are physically fit and active. But that's where the similarities end.

Where Liam's facial features are sharp and well defined, Devon's are softer. Devon's nose is also not as perfectly aligned as Liam's. Devon, having a short fuse and an urge to fight anyone who steps up to him, has had his nose broken a few times. The first break was from Tate, after Devon stole my first kiss and Tate took it upon himself to defend my honor.

I didn't bother to tell Tate that it was me who kissed Dev, but I doubt it would have mattered. Devon is Tate's best friend. Since my parents' deaths, Adrian and Tate both have treated me like a priceless doll, something to be handled with care, like I'll break at the slightest pressure. Therefore, Devon being older, no matter who instigated it, Devon was punished for the kiss.

I smile at Devon, those full lips of his in a deep scowl, and push my slice against the soft, plump flesh. "Why, you want some too?" I ask, not hiding the devious delight in my voice.

I'm in a special mood this morning. It's been nearly two years since I've been in the same room with the brothers. Papa's funeral was the last time, I believe. Back then, Liam and I had a secret fling going on, one that I'm sure his brother knows about. Devon may be Tate's best friend, but he's Liam's other half and they have never had a secret between them. They kept a secret from Tate, though.

That secret is me, and my secret is that I'd give all three of them every bit of my soul if they asked me.

"Fuck no." Devon pushes the pizza from his face. I shrug and take another bite of the slice.

"Your loss," I mumble through a mouthful of food. "So, where's Tate?"

Devon looks from me to Liam, who finally sits down next to his brother. The look they exchange tells me there's something I don't know. Something happened between last night and now.

"Where is Tate?" I ask again, setting the small bit of crust onto the top of the pizza box. "Liam, what happened?"

Liam sighs and refuses to look in my direction. He knows as well as I do he would tell me whatever it is I want to know. "Adrian had movers go to the apartment first thing this morning. The truck should be here with all your stuff soon," he says, avoiding my question.

Devon clears his throat, "Adrian also wants you to move your things into the master bedroom when they arrive. Kathleen is already shopping for groceries and new toiletries."

Devon stands up, looking anywhere but at his brother and me, and storms off out the door he came in from. I'm left dumbstruck, my mouth open slightly, my brain unable to form a rebuttal to the overly commanding last words. Instead of speaking, I snap my head to glare at Liam.

"Rhy, your apartment was vandalized after you left last night," Liam tells me. That bomb was unexpected. My heart speeds up. I had hoped the nightmare of last night would stay there, stay in the past, but that's probably too much to ask of fate.

"What?" I stammer. "I mean, how? How did you guys know?"

Liam slides over to the stool his brother had been in moments before. "Adrian got a call from the police station this morning. Some officers went by your apartment to ask you some follow-up questions and found the door open."

Fuck. Hot tears pool at the corners of my eyes. "Oh my god," I gasp. "If I—if I hadn't come here with Tate... oh my god."

"Nope. Don't even go there, Rhy." Liam wraps his arm around my shoulders and I rest my head against his chest. "You know damned well the three of us wouldn't let anything happen to you."

"You wouldn't have known. I still don't even know what Tate was doing at the apartment when he found me last night."

Before Liam can say anything for or against Tate's presence at my apartment, Devon comes back in. "The police are here. They want to speak with you, Rhyann."

The look on his face tells me he isn't in the mood for any bullshit or arguments from me. Not like I'd have anything to argue, anyway. This nightmare I've stumbled into feels unending.

"Fine, send them into my grandfather's study," I tell him, standing up and wiping the single tear that managed to escape my lashes.

Devon nods before turning on his heel and leaving me and Liam once again. I give Liam a sideways look, silently asking what's the matter with his twin. But I know. I know he's reliving the worst day of his life. The day the other part of the Morris trio was found dead.

"Let's go. I'll stay with you if you'd like." Liam holds out a hand and I take it with a quiet nod. "You know, it's not his study anymore. It's yours. This whole place belongs to you now," he reminds me as we leave the kitchen.

My grandfather's study is not what you'd picture for a man who ran a multi-million dollar company. I remember growing up thinking the room didn't fit with the rest of the house. Looking at it now, I see how it reflects the man that my grandfather was. The self-made businessman with a shrewd eye for finance.

The conservatively decorated room is still the same as it was when I was a kid. A simple desk made of metal with a frosted glass top. One wall holds a set of lacquered file cabinets where he kept important documents like birth and death certificates, stock information, and the deed to the house.

After he died, Adrian suggested I go through all the paperwork, but Papa's lawyer kept copies of everything. I just didn't see a point at the time. Now I guess I will have to make time.

"Miss Devereux. I hope you had a restful sleep last night," Crumpled Suit from last night greets me. The suit he wears now differs from the one I last saw him in. "My name is Detective David Myers."

He sets his business card down on the glass desktop. Liam picks up the small rectangular card and slips it into the back pocket of his jeans. "What can we do for you today, detective?" Liam asks for me.

I'm still in shock over my apartment being broken into. My mind keeps going back to the dark memory of being moved around last night, helpless and blindfolded. I wouldn't call myself a control freak, but the very thought of not being able to protect myself, the idea that someone could drug me, bind me, and sneak me out of my apartment—my safe space—is an icy spike to the heart. It's a crippling fear that I'm struggling to control.

"We'd like to ask Miss Devereux a few questions if that's okay, Mister...?" Crumpled Suit number two speaks up. He's also wearing a fresh set of clothes.

"Morris. Liam Morris." Liam extends his hand, but suit two doesn't take it. "And you are?"

"Detective Andrews. Can I ask what your relation to Miss Devereux is?" suit two, I mean Detective Andrews, asks, a scowl across his face.

"He's my—" I can't honestly finish my sentence. I don't even know what he is to me. Our relationship, if you want to call it that, is complicated at best.

"I'm her head of security," Liam finishes for me. I let out a long sigh of relief and look at him. Is this his way of asking for a job? I never cared much for the social workings of the elite, and I know his family has connections and money, so I doubt he needs a job.

"Well, I'm glad to see she has some sort of security detail, considering the circumstances," Detective Andrews says. "Now, where are Mister Crawford and his son?"

"I don't see why that matters," Liam answers. I give him a look. What is he hiding? He and Devon have both evaded my questions about Tate since I first asked over cold pizza. "Your concern is Miss Devereux and the attempted kidnapping, correct?"

"Yes, but," Detective Myers speaks up. "Tate Crawford was the one who found Miss Devereux, and we have a few questions for him as well."

"I'll let him know to get in touch with you when I see him," Liam assures the detectives.

The detectives nod, accepting Liam's compromise. I am not accepting some bullshit line like that, and will ask my own questions as soon as the detectives leave.

"Detectives, what happened at my apartment after I left?" I ask with a false bravado. If I let the men in this room think, even for a second, that I'm afraid, or incapable of handling the stress of this traumatic event, they will steam roll me and take my choices away. I won't let that happen again.

"Well, we aren't sure. The lock on the door was broken, and the apartment was wide open when we stopped by to ask questions this morning," Detective Myers explains. "Immediately we contacted Mister Crawford, and he informed us you were here."

"We were hoping you could come to the apartment and tell us if anything is out of place or missing," Detective

Andrews says with a callous coldness that says *I'm the bad cop here.*

"She will do no such thing. We've actually hired movers to clear out the apartment and bring her belongings here. She won't be returning there again," Liam responds.

Maybe it's my foggy brain from whatever was in my wine last night, but I just can't kick this feeling that they're hiding something from me. Speaking of last night... "Detectives, did the doctors determine what was in my wine last night?"

The two detectives look at each other before Detective Myers turns back to me. "The hospital sent a full report to Mister Crawford's email this morning. I'm surprised he hasn't updated you."

"I have yet to speak to Mister Crawford, or his son." I quirk my brow and glare in Liam's direction. He shrugs and leans back against the far wall. "So, if you don't mind, I'm sure you know the results. Do you mind sharing them with me? Seeing as how they pertain to *my* body."

"My apologies, Miss Devereux." Detective Myers clears his throat. "The toxicology shows that the wine was laced with some mild sedatives. Had you finished the second glass, it would have taken longer for you to wake up."

I swallow the knot in my throat. I don't know if this information is comforting or not. "And what about the kidnapper's identity?" I ask hesitantly.

"You see," Detective Andrew steps forward, placing both his boney hands on the frosted glass desktop separating us, "that's a bit of a conundrum, Miss Devereux. It seems that someone hasn't been truthful."

"Excuse me?" I stare at the arrogant asshole in front of me, his smug smile stretching the hollowness of his cheeks, creating tight folds over the corners of his mouth.

"Can you tell us again, when was the last time you saw or spoke with your father?" he asks, his thin chest puffing with pride.

"That's enough," Liam says in a voice I've never heard before. It's controlled violence and the promise of malice laced with something far darker.

"It's fine, Liam," I tell him, staring up into his face. My heart skips a beat and heat fills the valley between my thighs.

It's not the time to think about fucking your best friend's best friend, I tell myself.

"Detective, it's sad to see that you're sorely lacking in the skills required to do your job," I say as I watch Andrew's prideful expression morph into something of disgust and arrogant rage. "If you had done your jobs, you'd know the last time I saw my father was when I was ten." I lean forward, meeting the detective's gaze. "Why do you ask?"

"Rhyann," Liam says softly. He's moved to stand behind me. I can feel the heat radiate off his mountain of a body. He was there that day. The last time I saw my dad. "You don't have to talk to them. Your dad has nothing to do with this."

"On the contrary, Mister Morris. Her father is our prime suspect as of right now," Detective Dickhead—I mean Andrews– gloats.

"Impossible," I gasp.

"And why is that?" Detective Myers asks.

"Because the last time I saw my father, he was hanging from the ceiling fan in his office. He killed himself," I confess.

My head spins with confusion. A strong hand grips my arm and another holds my back as Liam guides me into the chair behind me. I can't tell if it's my body shaking or his hands, or both. But when I look up into his big beautiful eyes, his face is a reflection of the emotions coursing through my body. Both of us think back to that day, when a group of kids, ten and twelve years old, were playing hide and seek. The two of us sneaking into my father's office in search of the best hiding spot. What we found when we got there would haunt our dreams for years.

"Detectives, I think this interview is over," Liam says firmly.

"Wait!" I put my hand on his arm. "Why would my dead father be your prime suspect?"

Detective Andrew's once arrogant expression falters. "The trunk you were found in, the car is registered to Garret W. Montgomery."

And just like that, this nightmare couldn't get any worse.

"We'll be in touch, Miss Devereux," Detective Myers says sadly as he walks toward the door. "One more thing, Miss Devereux." I look up to meet the detective's eyes. "Why did you change your name from Devereux to Montgomery in school?"

"It was an orphan child's way of fitting in, Detective," I say quietly before the two of them leave.

Chapter 5

Liam

After the detectives arrived, Dev left for Rhyann's apartment. He knew she would not be okay with strangers packing up her life and moving everything without her. It was for the better anyway. It took all my strength to refrain from smashing the one guy's teeth in when he brought up her dad's suicide.

I can only imagine what my brother would have done when he saw Rhyann's face pale at their questions. It had to be me with her; it was me with her when she found him, so it was only natural it's me with her when the detectives questioned her about him.

No one else was there with her that day. No one else will ever understand what we walked into, the nightmares I know we both still have. It's a dark bond we share, a sinister rope tying us together from the time we were children to this very moment right here. The warmth of

Rhyann's hand on my arm radiates through me, thawing the icy rage inside.

Once the detectives leave, I take her hand in my own and begin kissing the tips of her fingers. One by one, I put each soft, small finger up to my lips just to feel the blood pulsing there—to remind myself she's really here. She's safe.

Last night, when Tate sent the text to my brother and me, I think my heart stopped for just a minute. I've loved Rhyann Devereux since the first moment I saw her. She was a princess holding court on the playground, and I wanted to be her knight in shining armor from that moment on.

"What are you doing?" Rhyann asks, pulling her small hand away.

"Reminding myself that you're real, and safe." I smile at her.

"Don't be weird," she laughs and slaps my cheek with her free hand. "Where did your brother run off to?"

Devon. My identical twin brother. Years ago, she gave her virginity to him. She never told anyone. Tate would have murdered my brother if he knew. She doesn't know that I know, though. She doesn't know that Devon and I have shared everything– every thought, every joy, every struggle– since the day our zygote formed in our mother's womb.

"And where has Tate been all day?" she throws in as an afterthought, although no one would ever call him that. That man is the center of her world. Always has been, always will be, and no matter how much my brother and I throw ourselves at her feet, we will never compare to him. He's preparing to pick his fiancee up from the airport tomorrow, though. Some Texas debutante whose father is a business associate of Adrian's. Soon to be Rhyann's, too. I'm not sure if that's the reason for his evasive attitude this morning, or if there's something he's hiding from us, but for whatever reason, he made me and Dev swear to secrecy about the fiancee thing. He doesn't want Rhyann to know, and I won't be the one to tell her.

"Who cares? It's just us today, let's enjoy it." I laugh and nibble the tip of her middle finger.

"Seriously Liam. knock it off. I told you we can't do this anymore." Rhyann sighs and pulls away from me. She turns to walk away, but I won't let go. Not this time, not ever again. My fingers tighten around her wrist and I pull her against my chest.

"Yeah, see, princess," I say slowly. "That's not gonna fly with me."

She clears her throat and swallows. Her green eyes sparkle as she bites her lower lip. With my free hand, I pinch her chin, pulling her wet lip from between her teeth. "Liam," she breathes.

My nostrils fill with the dizzying scent of cucumber and grapefruit. Fresh, inviting, comforting. My dick twitches against the heavy denim of my pants. Without thinking or caring, I close the distance between our lips. Her muffled protests are swallowed up in the heat of our kiss as I push with my tongue, begging her to open for me.

The second she does, that's all the permission I need. I lift her up and set her on the desk, pushing myself between her thighs, not once breaking the kiss.

The year her grandfather died, the year we spent together, we spent all our time in her apartment. Not once daring to have sex here, in this house. There were always too many ghosts, too many reminders of everyone she's lost. It's time to make new memories.

"I've fantasized about fucking you on this desk since I was in high school," I confess.

My rock hard cock pushes against my pants. She is home, she always has been, and my body recognizes that.

"I meant what I said, Liam. We can't do this anymore," she whispers back.

"If you don't want this," I pull away, resting my forehead against hers, "then by all means, push me away and walk out of the office."

When she doesn't push away immediately, I wrap my arm around her back. My hand cups the back of her head, fingers tangling in the beautiful mess of fiery red hair. My fingers close around her ginger strands and I pull her head back, exposing the length of creamy, pale flesh on her neck.

"Last chance, princess," I breathe against her skin as my lips trail down the side of her face, searching for the softest spot on her neck. "There's no going back from this, Rhyann."

"Liam," she moans my name when I find her pulse, flicking the delicate skin with my tongue.

I don't give her the chance to protest further. I claim her lips with my own in a hard kiss. One hand is still tangled in her hair, the other making its way up her soft thigh.

My fingers find the apex between her thighs and begin a soft, slow caress against the center of the thin black fabric of the leggings. God, I missed her. I missed her kiss, her scent. I missed the hot wetness I know is pooling between her legs as my nail grazes over her core.

Rhyann's hips shift and open wider, and she wraps her legs around my thighs. I pull her closer to me, replacing my hand with the rigid side of my erection. Her breath catches and she freezes when we make contact, but she finds her motion, grinding her clit against my cock.

"Fuck," I growl, nipping her bottom lip. I let go of her hair and my fingers make their way down her neck and arms. I cup a full, plump breast for a moment, letting its weight settle in my palm before both hands find their way to the waistband of her leggings.

She breaks our kiss, her head craning back, exposing her neck again for me. Her long red hair cascades down behind her like a fiery waterfall. I'm absolutely captivated by her, by the way her hips move, grinding against my cock. By her swollen, wet lips, open just enough for me to catch a glimpse of her velvety pink tongue as it grazes her teeth while she moans.

My own mouth aches for her, for a taste of her skin, her sweat and her juices. I take the opening and lean down, tasting the side of her neck. My tongue leaves a trail as I make my way to her breast.

Buzz...

THE SECRETS THAT WE KEEP   59

My back pocket starts to vibrate, sending a tingling sensation through my glutes, causing me to pause. I ignore it and continue to pinch Rhyann's hard little nipple between my teeth.

A throaty moan escapes her lips. The tinkling sound of a bell sounds off in the room.

"What's that?" Rhyann breathes out.

"Nothing," I growl, refusing to release her nipple from my teeth.

Just then, my phone vibrates in my pocket again as the ringing sound gets louder.

"Fuck," I pull away just slightly. "It's our phones."

"That's not exactly nothing," she says, looking for her phone on the desk.

My own phone vibrates in my pants once more and with an annoyed sigh, I pull it out.

"What?" I growl into the speaker.

"Quit trying to dip your dick in holes it doesn't belong in," Devon laughs on the other end. It isn't an amused laugh. No, we've been at odds since I told him about me and Rhyann a year ago. "Let me in. I'm at the front door."

"This won't happen again," Rhyann says as I hang up with my brother. She doesn't bother looking at me as she says the words. "I hate you, Liam." She just walks out of the study, her eyes focused on the screen of her phone.

Chapter 6

Rhyann

"Now, what the fuck are the two of you not telling me?" I ask the twins as we oversee the unloading of the moving van. My entire life over the past two years fit perfectly into the back of a small U-Haul.

When Devon showed back up at the house, I insisted on going to the apartment to pack my own clothes. My justification was not wanting someone I didn't know touching my underwear. Both brothers bought the excuse, although they maintained their stance on me not returning to my apartment.

They also refuse to tell me where Tate has been all day. So, here we are now, at an impasse. I am not letting up on the topic. After two years of no contact, Tate shows up just in time to rescue me from an attempted kidnapping, just to disappear the next morning. Totally not suspicious.

"No clue. What do you mean?" Devon avoids looking in my direction.

"Why are you even here, Devon?" I ask, frustrated with the passive aggressive attitude he has given me all day. When Liam snorts with laughter, I turn to glare at him. "And you! What the fuck? You are not my Head of Security." I make air quotes with my fingers.

"Actually, princess, I am." Liam's jovial tone turns deep, dominant.

God, I hate the way his voice can invoke the most salacious thoughts. I have to take a deep breath and focus on my anger to get through the argument I know I'm about to have.

"No," I pinch the bridge of my nose. "You're not. You were hired to install a security system, not be my personal bodyguard. If I need security, I will hire someone. Now, will you both please leave. I've had enough of the lies and secrets today."

I turn back to the house. The movers are well paid, so I'm confident they can do their job without being babysat by a couple overbearing men and a woman with trust issues. "Let's go," I hear Devon tell his brother. "If she wants to put herself at risk, we can't stop her."

I don't say anything as I return to the house. I don't hear Liam's response, but when I ask Kathleen to look out the window and check if they're still out there, I'm a little sad when she says no.

Kathleen was so happy to have me back home, to have someone to care for, that she made all my favorite foods for dinner. I'm not talking about just my favorite dinner dishes. No. She made french toast with powdered sugar, grilled cheese and tomato soup, and chicken and dumplings. For dessert, she made strawberry shortcake and the biggest apple pie I've ever seen.

I don't know how she expected me to eat all this food, but somehow between me, her, and Phil, we finished off all the french toast and most of the tomato soup. The chicken and dumplings and the dessert all went into the fridge for tomorrow's leftovers.

Before the two of them left, I promised to sit down with her later this week to figure out how we are going to manage the estate now that I'm going to be living here for the foreseeable future.

It's a lonely feeling, sitting in this big house, alone for the first time. When I would come home for the summers, and Papa would go to whatever charity event or dinner party, leaving me behind, I loved it. It was different back then. I knew he would be back, and the emptiness of the place was thrilling.

Now, I feel like I need to lock every door of every room I walk into. Every sound, every moan or groan of the wood, or the whistling of the wind as it blows through the property, makes the hair on my neck stand on end.

Before Phil left, he and Kathleen helped me go through the boxes that covered the floor of the four-car garage. It used to hold cars. Papa had a love for classic cars. When he died, I sold most of them to collectors. I kept my favorite, though. A cherry red 1965 Shelby Mustang GT350. It's currently in storage in the city.

I drove it the first six months after Papa died, then some dick wad in the University parking lot decided not to pay attention and dinged the paint job with his car door. Since then, I've been afraid to drive her. *I should bring her home*, I think with a sigh.

I'm almost finished with unpacking the last box. It's pretty much small stuff, like my makeup, perfumes, and

THE SECRETS THAT WE KEEP

hair care products. My clothes and other personal, more private items, I packed myself between my two suitcases.

I roll my head from side to side, popping my neck. I'm not sure how long I've been sitting in this spacious bedroom, going through boxes, but my muscles ache and I need a drink. I stand up and reach down to touch my toes, stretching my legs, then I bend in the opposite direction, my hands on my hips, until I feel my back pop.

Kathleen stocked the wine fridge this afternoon and the pantry, kitchen, and the fridge in the game room. I already planned to give her a raise, but when she came back with a literal truckload of food and supplies for the house, I told her I was going to triple her wages, and I meant it. I've already emailed the estate's lawyer, instructing him to triple both hers and Phil's wages. After I booted the guys from the property today, I sent him another email about setting up interviews for security detail, as well as adding some additional staff to help lighten the load for Phil and Kathleen.

I debate opening a bottle of cab that Kathleen bought this morning, but the thought of wine sends a little bolt of panic through me, and I opt for the kitchen and a bottle of water. The kitchen is dark, but there's enough moonlight coming in from the small square windows above the sink that I don't bump into the counter on my way to the Sub-Zero fridge.

After I grab two bottles of water, one for now and another for later tonight—so I don't have to come back downstairs in the dark—I turn around and scream. Both bottles drop to the floor in my shock.

"Why did you kick Liam and Devon out today?" Tate's voice cuts through the darkness like a knife.

Clutching my chest, I take several deep breaths to steady my heart. "Jesus Christ, Tate. You scared me."

"Answer me, Rhy. Don't you care about your own safety?" His voice is low, his words slowed and slurring just a tad.

"You're drunk," I tell him, looking down to see if I can find the two lost bottles of water. "Besides, where were you all day?"

"I was trying to protect you, Rhyann. Something you don't seem too concerned with doing for yourself." Tate takes a couple of steps toward me, backing me up against the fridge.

"Protect me from what?" I ask.

"From me, stupid." Before I can react to that, before I can ask him what the hell he means, he has a hand around my neck, pinning me in place, and he leans down and slams his lips against mine.

The kiss is unexpected, and hard. It's hot and needy. I want to fight it; I know I should. But something in me wants this, needs this. The velvet soft tip of his tongue teases my lips, and I open for him. A moan escapes my throat, vibrating his grip on me.

"I've been thinking about you all afternoon, beautiful," Tate growls against my lips. Although he's significantly taller than me, Tate and I are a perfect fit, our bodies locking like pieces of a puzzle. His woodsy sandalwood and bourbon scent fills my nostrils.

"Tate, what are you doing?" I huff out. My body presses against the wall of his chest, my tits smashed tightly between us.

His hand slides down my side, softly touching my breasts, then the dips in my waist before digging into my hips. "My god, Rhy." His voice is hoarse, pained. "You have no idea how hard it's been to keep my hands off you."

"Well, you're doing a shit job of controlling yourself right now." I push my hips out, grinding my mons against his groin. Tate has a one-track mind when he drinks, and that track is sex. Always was and always will be sex.

My movements earn me a moan as Tate relaxes into me. My fingers dig into his hard chest and I push him back. I stretch up on my toes so we can be eye to eye. "Well, Tate. Are you going to hurt me? Do you want to punish me?"

My whole body shakes with adrenaline. Tate has pushed me to the edge of desire and hatred so many times, I'm ready to dive head first, damn the jagged soul-crushing rocks at the bottom.

"Rhyann, you have no idea the things I want to do to you," Tate growls.

"What if I want to know?" I take a step forward, my hands gripping the fabric of his shirt.

"Nothing good will come from this," he warns, his hand reaching up, cradling the back of my head. His strong fingers tangle in the mess of my red hair.

I laugh softly. It's a desperate, lonely sound. "My life is nothing but a series of tragedies, Tate. What's it going to hurt to add one more to the list?"

"My Rhyann," Tate whispers before claiming my mouth once again. He wraps his arms around me, closing the little bit of distance that remained. With almost no effort, Tate lifts me off the ground and turns us, setting me down on the marble countertop.

Tate's lips trail down the side of mouth and find the soft flesh of my ear. My nails scrape down his chest, searching for the hem of his shirt while he pulls my earlobe between his teeth. The tip of his tongue teases and tastes the bit of flesh before moving on to taste the rest of my neck.

My fingers fiddle with the hem of his shirt, finding their way to the firm spread of muscles at his waist. I can't recall ever touching Tate like this. Whenever we were together growing up, he treated me more like the kid sister he never wanted, or the best friend he couldn't stand to be away from, but never has he kissed me, or touched me like he is now.

His mouth finds its way down to my chest, just above the camisole I'm wearing for pajamas. My full double-D cups are sitting free of the bra that traps them daily, my nipples hard little pebbles poking through the satin. My hands travel up his abdomen to the splash of hair at his chest as Tate's free hand makes its way between my thighs.

Two fingers push the crotch of my matching satin shorts and lace panties aside, exposing the hot, slick folds of my pussy to the night air. I moan into the darkness as Tate slides his fingers between my lips at the same time as he bites down on a satin covered nipple.

"Fuck," I cry.

"Mmm," Tate moans around my tit.

He pumps his hand in and out of my pussy, my juices dripping out to pool on the cold marble beneath me. Tate lifts his head, my top soaked where his mouth was, leaving my breast chilled in the night air.

"Rhyann," he breathes, looking me in the eye before claiming my mouth fast and hard for another kiss.

"Tate, please," I beg, fighting the needy tears that are pooling at the rims of my eyelids. My hips slide forward on the counter, my clit grinding into his hand.

Even if it hadn't been close to a year since I've had sex, this moment, the carnal need to be touched by Tate, to be consumed by him, loved by him, is something I've been fighting against for as long as I can remember. I'm tired of fighting. I don't want to lie to myself anymore. I'm sick of the secrets I've kept, even from myself.

"I need you," I admit to the both of us in the dark. I reach for the button of his pants and he pushes my hand away.

"Shh," Tate whispers against my mouth when I begin to protest his denial. Before I can say anything else, Tate breaks the kiss and bends down in front of me. Both his hands grip my hips and he pulls me to the edge of the counter.

He slips first one leg over his shoulder and then the next. Soft, warm lips trail butterfly light kisses between both my legs from the knee all the way to the now sopping wet fabric at my crotch.

My hands slide behind me and my breath hitches. "Oh god," I breathe.

Tate chuckles, his mouth firmly against the inside of my thigh. Thank god the artery is too deep for him to feel my speeding pulse. He continues his trail of kisses, though, alternating from one leg to the other until his tongue reaches my core.

Tate pulls at my shorts and underwear from the wet fabric in the center, sliding them down my legs and dropping them on the floor. With nothing but a deep growl as a warning, Tate claims my womanhood with his mouth.

His kiss is soft and sweet, and I can't say I've ever been kissed like that, not on those lips, at least. That's the only tenderness he shows me- it's as if he's thanking the Greek goddess of pleasure, Hedone, for the feast he's about to devour.

And my god—or should I say goddess—does he deliver. As soon as his show of tenderness is over, his mouth begins its assault. First, he drags his tongue up the length of my seam, from the soft stretch of flesh between my the pucker of my ass, up to my clit. When he reaches the apex, he pulls my swollen little bean into his mouth.

I let out a moan as he traps my clit gently between his teeth and flicks his tongue over the sensitive flesh. Tate releases the hold with his teeth but doesn't break the suction with his lips. The assault with his tongue continues over my nerves while he suckles. One hand leaves my hips and two fingers slide between my engorged lips.

He pumps his fingers, fucking me with his hand, never once breaking his hold on my clit. My body trembles with the building tension as my hips rock back and forth, matching the rhythm he's created with his fingers and his tongue.

"Tate. Oh god," I breathe. "I'm gonna cum."

"Mmmhmm," he moans over my clit. That subtle vibration sets off the most exquisite fireworks display behind my eyes as I lean back and let the orgasm take over my entire body.

THE SECRETS THAT WE KEEP   73

My bare feet dig into his shoulders, and my body succumbs to tremors. "Tate," I grind out between gritted teeth. "Fuuuck."

After a few seconds, the tremors subside, but Tate continues, his tongue replacing his fingers as he laps up my juices. He places a soft kiss on the inside of my thigh and stands to face me.

In the silver glow of the moon, I can see the glistening sheen of my cum coating his lips and chin. I steady myself and grab a fist full of his shirt, pulling him against me. The ridge of his rock hard cock pushes at my now hyper-sensitive lady bits. The remaining wetness and juices soak the front of his pants as I kiss his lips, sucking the bottom one into my mouth and lapping up the tangy saltiness of my cum.

My hips roll, grinding my clit against the abrasive fabric covering his erection. "Please," I moan against his mouth.

"I can't." The tone in his voice is pained, sorrowful, invoking a sinking feeling in the pit of my stomach.

"Tate," I say, letting go of his shirt, searching for his face in the moonlight.

"I'm sorry Rhy. I warned you." He backs away from me, turning to the back door. "I was getting ready for my fiancee to come to town. That's where I was all day."

Tate drops the bomb that obliterates my already fragile little universe and leaves me sitting half naked in the dark.

Chapter 7

Rhyann

I sit at the kitchen counter, snacking on some grapes and scrolling through my phone. I've decided I'm going to take a vacation. I emailed the lawyer this morning. I know it wasn't a stipulation in my grandfather's will for me to intern at Devereux Publications, but I want to check with him just in case there's any question or doubt from Adrian.

I also sent Adrian a text, asking if he would meet me for lunch. He was MIA all day yesterday. Likely rubbing elbows with his soon to be daughter-in-law and her family. My face contorts into a scowl at the thought of Tate and this mystery woman. Although, do I really have a right to judge? It's not like we have anything more than a long time off and on friendship.

If anything, we should be more like siblings than friends or lovers. Small cracks form in my heart. The thought of us being lovers—or never being lovers—invokes memories of what we almost had last night.

The scent of sandalwood and bourbon, his mouth over my clit, suckling and pulling the orgasm from my body. Fuck. I moan, sucking a crisp grape into my mouth.

"Grapes that good?"

"What the fuck!" I yell. My soul might have jumped from my body when Dev's bulky frame entered my line of vision.

"Jumpy much, princess?" He laughs at the stunned expression on my face. Why is he here? What's changed about his shit attitude from yesterday? Maybe he went and got himself fucked hard, too.

"I thought I told you and your brother to get lost." I push off the barstool. Its legs skid across the tile floor of my open kitchen. *My kitchen!* I did it! I remembered that this is my motherfucking house now! My hands grip the edge of the counter, holding me in place. This is my home now, my space, and he has no business being here without my consent.

"You did, and Adrian has his own opinions about that, little girl." Where Tate and I have danced around the sexual tension in our relationship for years, and Liam and I have indulged in it, Devon and I have constantly battled with open disdain for each other ever since he was drunk at sixteen and confessed his deepest secret to me.

"Well, Adrian can come here and discuss those plans with me, not send his son's idiot best friend to harass me and raid my pantry." I scowl as Devon opens the fridge.

"Oh, trust me. He plans to." He grins, pulling out the ingredients necessary for a turkey sandwich. "But right now, he asked us to help Phil with setting up your new security system."

He gloats as he pulls a small gray business card from his pocket, slapping it on the counter in front of me. I look down and read the embossed gold writing:

Morris Brothers Private Security and Alarm

Oh, god. That means...

"Well, hello, beautiful." Liam's gentle, hypnotic voice rings out behind me. His blue eyes sparkle behind long, full lashes. His shaggy blonde hair doing its own thing. My fingers tingle, remembering how it felt to run them through those blonde tresses.

"Why you guys?" I groan.

"Because we're the best." Liam's smile could light the entire house, it's so bright.

"How did you get in here?" I glare at Devon.

He laughs, lifts one of his hands, twirling a ring on his index finger with a single silver key attached. Fuck.

Liam drops the boxes in his arms on the counter beside me. "What's the matter? Didn't you miss me?"

He's so close. His big hands rest next to mine. I have a death grip on the edge of the counter. But my eyes are glued to Devon. I know how to deal with Liam, and I can handle Tate. But there's this fire behind Devon's blue eyes, a war stirring in him that scares the shit out of me. Because I know, without a doubt, whatever it is that's brewing in him will explode in an epic mess that somehow I will be at the center of.

I don't think he notices me staring. He's just standing there humming to himself, making a sandwich in my kitchen like he fucking owns the place.

"Are you thinking about me, princess?" Devon's lips curl into a wicked smile, his blue eyes alight with a promise of words that I know would leave me in tears for the rest of the day. But we aren't teens anymore. We aren't in high school. He can't hurt me anymore. I hope.

"Thinking of shoving you over the railing out there." I nod to the door leading to the foyer and the aforementioned balcony at the top of the stairs. "Wanna check out the view with me?"

Liam quietly unboxes all the new security equipment, observing the back and forth between Dev and me.

"Oh. I see; you just want to get me alone." Dev's sinister smile doesn't waver as he lifts the mayonnaise and mustard-coated butter knife to his mouth, wiping it down the surface of his velvety pink tongue, and winks at me.

He fucking winked at me. Liam lets out a low laugh, and I turn and glare at him. He shrugs and blows me a kiss. What is wrong with them? You'd think they would act like grown-ups at their age. You'd think, after years of this shit, they'd get bored and leave me alone.

"I hate you," I seethe and turned to leave the room. "Both of you."

TATE

"Shit, man. How long has she been in there?" Dev asks, one hand on my shoulder, the other holding his Hydro Flask.

"Close to an hour." I groan. We spent many days as kids playing pool in Rhyann's grandfather's game room. She spent so much time there that she became a pool shark by the time she was fifteen. There wasn't a person who walked into this house that could beat her. "Her music choice has been interesting, too."

"The Devil Within" by Digital Daggers is the current song she's blasting through her Bluetooth speaker.

"I have a feeling she's trying to send a message." I laugh.

After she left the kitchen, Rhyann stomped off into the game room. I figured she went into the office, or her room, until I heard the music coming from the opposite end of the house. The first song she put on was "Weaker Girl" by Banks. I followed the sound and watched

THE SECRETS THAT WE KEEP   81

from the doorway as she racked the balls, chalked up her favorite cue, and lined up her shot. I didn't think she'd notice me watching, but then she set her cue down and gave me a double "fuck you" with both her middle fingers.

I wasn't supposed to be here. I was supposed to be picking my fiancee up from the airport. The fiancee that I would give anything to not have to marry. But I couldn't resist stopping in on my way. I needed to make sure Rhyann was okay, that she wasn't driving the guys absolutely insane while they did what my father hired them to do.

When we were kids growing up, Rhyann's innocence fascinated me. She was so sweet and feisty. Devon would pick on her when he and Liam came over to play, but she quickly stuck up for herself. She found a friend in Gemma, the twins' only sister, and the five of us became a team. Yeah, we teased the girls often, and I made the twins swear that they'd never hurt Rhyann. Even back then, I felt a sense of protectiveness over her that I still can't explain.

After her parents died—first her mom, then her dad a year later— she changed. She withdrew into herself, and I was afraid I was going to lose my ginger-haired soulmate.

She's always been and always will be a part of me. As though we were destined to be a part of each other's lives since before we were born.

Well, of course we were; all of our parents were best friends. It was only natural that we would have a bond from day one. Yet I can never let Rhyann know how deep that bond goes. How I have this unhealthy need to be close to her always. Watching her, protecting her, never right there with her, but never far away, either.

Until the end of this month, that is. After I marry Aubree, it would be the ultimate sign of disrespect to both women to continue my obsession—that's basically what I have with Rhyann, an obsession. I can't breathe, I can't think, I can't begin to comprehend life without Rhyann.

"When does the plane land?" Devon asks, clearing my head. Aubree insisted on staying in Texas with her mother and stepfather until the last minute. She said she can't stand California and thinks everyone here are vegan hippies who hate everything they disagree with.

"Four p.m." I shrug. "It's a non-stop flight, she hasn't even left Texas yet."

"When do you plan on telling her?" Dev asks. I assume he's referring to Rhyann. He's as protective of her as I

THE SECRETS THAT WE KEEP   83

am. I still don't know what happened between the two
of them the year Liam and I went to college, but things
changed between them. She hates him with a passion,
and all he wants to do is protect her, even from me.

Liam and I both went to college right out of high-
school. It was the only thing that saved him from the
pain of losing his sister the year before. Dev stayed home
that summer and made sure his mother was going to be
okay. I know that was the last summer he and Rhyann
spent together as friends. From what my father told me,
he was here damned near every day, protective pseudo
big brother, always making sure she was safe and never
lonely.

"I don't," I say without looking my best friend in the
eyes. I don't need to see the expression on his face to know
he wants to beat my ass right now. "It's not like she'll care,
anyway."

"You're a fucking moron, you know that?"

I nod. "You think she and Liam will get together?" The
idea of anyone with Rhyann hurts, but if I have to watch
someone love her and take care of her, I'd rather it be one
of the twins.

"They think we don't know they've been seeing each other for the past four years," Devon smirks. "I'm going to bring it up to my brother tonight."

"Please wait until after you meet Aubree," I ask with a sigh. The two of them rarely fight, but when they do, it affects everyone.

The last time they fought was the fall after Rhyann's grandfather died. Liam was angry at Devon for something that happened between him and Rhyann years before. Whatever it was that made Rhyann despise Devon almost ruined the bond between the brothers. Because we had all grown up together, it was painful to watch and nearly destroyed the friendships I had with the two of them.

"Think she'll forgive me for what happened years ago?" Devon breaks the silence.

"Depends. What the fuck happened between the two of you?" I ask, trying not to let my annoyance show. That's the one thing Devon has never confided in me. The one thing that would probably destroy our friendship.

"What does it matter? It's in the past." Devon says. "Shit, you're getting married. You can't hold on to

Rhyann forever, man. It's only going to hurt her, and your fiancee."

Devon has a point. Why can't I let her go? Why can't I just walk away from Rhyann, let her have the life she deserves? Be with the man she wants to be with. That's one reason I wasn't planning to be here today. "Old habits die hard, I guess?"

"Well, whatever you do, I have your back. Always. Just don't fucking hurt her."

My shoulders relax, and Dev and I leave Rhyann to her angry game against herself.

Out in the spacious living room, Liam's packing up his tools and the empty boxes from the brand-new equipment he just finished installing.

"How's our favorite troublemaker doing?" he asks.

Liam loved torturing her as a kid. He's the one who nicknamed her Red. She hated it back then, and I would be surprised if she grew to like it now. We all knew from day one that Liam was in love with her. But he respected my boundaries, respected the fact that I didn't want them dating her. So, he let her go; he dated his sister's friends and even made his way through the cheerleading squad in high school.

But whenever Rhyann tried to talk to one of the local boys when she came home for the summers, Liam was right there to scare them off. He was extremely possessive of her back then. The one time someone did show interest in Rhyann, Liam went wild. He broke the guy's nose for taking her to the movies and made sure that no other guy so much as looked at her.

"She's fine. Are you finished?" I ask. Having her home and so close grated at me for some reason. Sure, I enjoyed teasing her, and I think Liam and his crush are entertaining, but something about the whole situation with Rhyann and the almost kidnapping has me on edge. It's like the universe was trying to tell me to change my path, because as we're helping Liam clear the mess from the installation, "Gasoline" by Halsey starts playing in the back of the house. It's time to go.

Chapter 8

Rhyann

I leave the guys to do the job Adrian hired them to do and walk into the game room. I'm not surprised this time when I spot Tate lurking in the doorway. Watching me. Fucker. What the hell does he think is going to happen after what he did, what he said last night?

I hate him, but I don't hate him. Not really, not at all. The truth is I'm heart broken, shattered. I never imagined there'd be anything between us, but I never imagined I'd have to give him up to someone else either.

I'm trying my hardest not to throw my cell phone across the room and into the wall as I stab my finger at the screen, calling Adrian up.

"Rhyann, is everything okay?" Adrian answers on the first ring.

Deep breaths, Rhy. Deep fucking breaths. I take two deep breaths before speaking to the man who has been like an uncle to me for my entire life. "Actually, yes."

"Go on," Adrian says when I collect my thoughts.

"Well, I'd appreciate it if you stopped making decisions for me, Adrian." It's a test of my strength to keep my tone even. "I'm turning twenty-five in less than a year. I'm not a child anymore."

"I'm sorry Rhyann. You're right," Adrian says. There's a rustling and a muffle of sounds on his end of the line.

"Have I interrupted you, Adrian? We can discuss this later."

He laughs softly. I've always enjoyed his laugh. It's comforting and jovial. "Actually, I just pulled into the driveway. I have a surprise for you. Why don't you come out and see."

I don't say anything, I just end the call and run through the hall and out of the house. I step out into the warm California sun and gasp. My hands go to my mouth and I fight back tears of joy.

"Donna!" I squeal. Yes, I named my car Donna. It's the perfect name for a classic beauty. "Adrian, how did you know?" I walk slowly, approaching my beautiful cherry

THE SECRETS THAT WE KEEP   89

red Mustang with the care and caution someone would approach an actual mustang.

"Well, I knew she was in storage because you were at school. I just had a hunch that you wanted her home with you." He smiles and shrugs his shoulders like it's no big deal.

But having Donna home, having my car here with me, is a huge deal. It's the biggest deal. Just looking at my beautiful girl cuts some of the lingering bitter emotions that have been chasing me since Tate stormed out last night. "Thank you," I cry, throwing my arms around Adrian's neck.

"You're welcome," he laughs, rubbing my back between my shoulder blades. "Why don't we take the old girl for a drive, grab lunch, and talk like you wanted?"

"I'd really like that." I smile and run into the house to grab my purse and a pair of flip-flops. The twins see me run through the house like a madwoman, and when Devon makes a snide comment, I give him my middle finger on my way back out.

Adrian tosses me the keys and slides into the passenger seat. God, I missed Donna. I missed the smell of gasoline and old leather. I missed the rumble of the V-8 engine under the hood. It's a cathartic feeling to be encased in so much power.

"So, Tate told you about Aubree." It's more of a statement to break the silence than a question. I keep my eyes on the road.

"He told me he's engaged," I confirm.

"I think you'll like her, Rhyann." Adrian gives me a soft smile.

"That's good. I'm happy for Tate no matter what." I don't push Donna to her limits, like I want to. Not with Adrian in the car. I try not to show any emotion at all right now. Adrian, and even Papa, have treated me delicately my whole life.

We drive over the San Mateo bridge with the windows down. It's a beautiful day, the water calm below us, and the sky as blue as Liam's and Devon's eyes. My favorite shade of blue.

I sigh. I get why Liam is on my mind. After what happened last night with Tate, maybe what I need is a good, hard fuck from Liam. But Devon... I can't get the broken, sad look in his eyes out of my head.

Adrian and I eat lunch at a small bistro in Redwood City, overlooking the bay. It's a nice quiet lunch. The first time the two of us have ever sat and talked. Outside of work, that is. I told him how I think I need a vacation. He agrees and assures me that there is nothing to worry about regarding the conditions of my inheritance.

As far as the money goes, the estate itself, I've had that since Papa died. The business, Devereux Publications, is what I worry about.

"Rhyann," Adrian says in his comforting father-like tone. "Your grandfather would not want you stressing on the company like this."

"I know," I sigh. "I just want to make him proud, and it's not like I have much of a social life." I shrug, looking out over the bay.

"Oh honey." Adrian takes my hand in his. "You made him proud a long time ago. You continue to make him proud every day. If you need a break, take a break. Devereux Publications isn't going anywhere."

"Thank you Adrian," I say.

We sit like this for a while. Both of us staring out into the stillness of the bay. On the way home, I let Adrian drive Donna. I just want to enjoy the ride, let the wind blow through my hair, and pretend my world is perfect.

But the fantasy only lasts so long because there are important things we need to talk about. I tell him about what the detectives said. That the car Tate found me in is registered to my father, or someone using his name. He nods and tells me they gave him that information the other night, when I was in shock over having almost been kidnapped. That explains the conversation outside the apartment.

Adrian also explains that the police were concerned about sexual assault and, since I had been drugged, they thought a rape kit would be ideal. That's why he insisted on a private room. Which went to waste because I put my foot down. Something Adrian was proud of.

Then Adrian tells me what I've really needed to hear throughout all this. He tells me he's sorry for not giving me the chance to make the big decisions for myself. I'm a grown woman and it's time for him to treat me like one.

By the time we arrive back at my house, I'm in tears. I tell Adrian that I've always looked to him as a father and am grateful for his guidance before he leaves me to my big empty house. A house with too many ghosts and too many memories.

I told Kathleen not to worry about food or cleaning for the rest of the weekend, so the house should be empty by now. I pull my keys from my purse and am about to unlock the front door when I see a keypad with ten numbers on it, and no keyhole.

For the love of god. I swear, the Morris brothers are fucking with me. I toss the useless house key back into my purse and grab my phone. I send a quick text to Liam and wait for a reply.

It's Devon who answers me, though.

Devon: Sorry princess. Forgot to give you your new lock code. It's 1028. See ya soon.

Well, it would be great if I could pick the code myself. Fuck that! I dial the number that texted me.

"Yes, princess?" The noise in the background is almost loud enough to drown out the person on the phone. I can barely make out Devon's voice.

"Fuck you, dickhead. How do I reset it?"

It suddenly goes quiet on his end and I hear him laugh. "Reset what?"

Ugh! I squeeze my phone. I want to break something. He's fucking with me. "The fucking code. I don't want you idiots having my lock code."

"No can do, dollface," another voice chimes in. "My dad paid for the full service package, which includes 24/7 monitoring of your home. Contractually, we as a company cannot enter your home, but do have access in the event of an emergency."

What the ever loving fuck? Adrian wouldn't have signed me up for some Big Brother *1984* bullshit. There's no way. He's my next call.

"Bullshit." I call their bluff. "I'll just hire a new company to remove your lock and replace it with my own."

"Good luck." Devon laughs as I end the call.

I can't believe the arrogance of those men. I send a text to Adrian asking him about having the locks changed. The house is quiet, as usual, when I walk inside. I'm not sure I'll ever get used to being in such a large place by myself. After this whole kidnapping ordeal is settled, maybe I should sell the house. Maybe I could give it to Tate and his fiancee as a wedding gift.

Hot, angry tears threaten to spill down my cheeks. I just ate a great lunch, but my stomach is as empty as this big house. I hate it here. I think I always have. I stay because it's the only thing connecting me to my past. A past that at this moment, I'd love nothing more than to forget.

I toss my phone into the big bed in the middle of my bedroom and get the steam shower going in the bathroom. One thing is certain, my grandfather had great taste. He had an acute eye for detail. I'm about to step into the tile shower stall when my phone dings on the bed. I sigh and close the glass door and walk back into my room, barefoot and naked. I already know it's Adrian before I look at the screen.

Adrian: Rhyann, it's your house. Of course you can do what you want. But I know the boys have your best interest at heart. They should have stayed to show you how to run your own system. I'll talk to them.

I groan, mildly disappointed at his response. However, I'm not all that surprised. It is my decision to make, thank you, Adrian. Are you sure the boys have my best interest in mind? It seems to me they're self serving control freaks who seem to think I'm some sort of pet for them to take out and play with whenever they feel the urge.

But I don't say that to Adrian. I don't text him and tell him how his son showed up last night and tongue fucked me on the kitchen counter before dropping the engagement bomb on me and dipping out before I could respond. Nope. I don't say anything that I want to say.

Rhyann: Thank you. I appreciate that.

His next response is almost immediate. It's as though he was waiting for me to text him back.

Adrian: Also, I would feel more confident if you let Liam handle your security. At least until we find out who tried to kidnap you, and why.

Well, there's that. Fuck.

Rhyann: Fine.

I send my text and throw the phone across the room, this time not caring one bit if it breaks or damages the wall. The patter of the water from the shower is the only thing that seems to keep me from screaming at the top of my lungs right now.

I take a deep breath and allow the call of the water to draw me in. Once there, I slide down to the shower floor, hugging my knees to my chest and resting the back of my head against the wall behind me.

By the time my parents were my age, they were happily married and living their best lives. My mom was working for Papa at Devereux Publications, and my dad was chasing whatever dreams he had. It's kind of sad, if I think about it, but I don't know what my dad did for work. I know he had a college degree because that's where he met my mother. In college.

THE SECRETS THAT WE KEEP   97

Past that, all I really know about either of my parents
was that they loved each other fiercely. Mom loved me,
and it was difficult when she got sick, and then died. But
my father loved her more than he loved anyone else in this
world, even me. He couldn't imagine a world without
her in it. I know, because that's one of my last memories
of him.

I'll never forget that night. He had just moved us back
in with Papa, insisting that it was better for us to be close
to family. Really, he knew what he was going to do and
didn't want me to be alone. He tucked me into bed that
night, kissing me on the forehead and telling me that
there is no life worth living if there isn't love in it. I went
to sleep that night thinking my father loved me, and woke
up just to find out the only person he would ever love was
my mother, the one person who left him the year before.

He was right, though. Life is painful and lonely without love, without someone to share it with. The joys
and the sorrows, the pains and the pleasures. None of
it means anything if you're doing it alone. My life isn't
worth the money it's been built on.

The expensive private school, the fancy college, even
this big empty house. It's all been wasted on me, on

someone who has struggled to fit in, to make friends, to make personal connections with others.

It's not like I haven't tried, haven't put myself out there, laid myself bare and raw to my peers. I have. I've done it all, everything I can do to make friends, to build relationships with others. I've dated, I've gone out for drinks with my college roommates and co-workers. I've even gone as far as swapping phone numbers and exchanging Instagram profiles with a handful of people.

In the end, I can just tell. People have an inherent way of choosing their friends. It's obvious from the first impression if you and the other person will mesh well, if you'll become the best of friends or if you're destined to watch each other's lives unfold over a series of posts on social media, your only interactions a like on a picture or post and throwing the occasional *YAS!* or *Slay Queen!* into the comments here and there.

My grandfather sent me to Evangeline's to protect me, give me a stability he couldn't give me as a child. I think he hoped I'd make friends, quit isolating myself from the rest of the world and make the emotional connections my father couldn't make with his peers.

I remember little about both of my parents, but I know they were like night and day. My mother was vivacious and bright. She was friendly and everyone she came in contact with automatically wanted to be her friend. My father, on the other hand. He was quiet, kept his circle small, and did his best to avoid crowded social functions and people he didn't know.

Tears roll down my cheeks, getting caught in the corners of my mouth. I know they're tears because when the tip of my tongue swipes at my lips, I taste the hot saltiness of my emotions.

I always thought I was like my father, having a close circle of friends in Tate, the twins, and Gemma. Even after I was sent to Evangeline's, Gemma and the guys kept in touch. They'd text me daily, and even send the best care packages. But, even before Gemma died, things started to change between all of us. Gemma texted and wrote less. When I would call on the weekends, she was busy with the friends she made at her school, friends her own age, and the guys were off sticking their dicks in one hole or another.

After she died, our relationships whenever I was home went from having the adventures of a lifetime to a passing greeting whenever we were forced to be in the same room.

I don't know how long I sit under the water, my tears blending with the water falling on my skin. But when I step out of the shower, my fingers and toes are covered in wrinkles. I towel dry my hair and wrap myself in the same purple robe from the other night. I like the way it feels against my bare skin. It's a soft terry cloth, so it absorbs water and feels good as I move.

I still haven't unpacked all my clothes, so I go straight for the stack of suitcases on the floor of the walk-in closet. I dig through a couple of them, looking for clean clothes. Fresh underwear and socks. I grab a new bra, just in case my phone is broken and I have to go back out before the stores close.

I'm sifting through the mess of fabric when my finger brushes against a velvet bag. I smile to myself and pull the bag up from the mess. I almost forgot that I packed my favorite vibrator in my suitcase rather than one of the boxes with my other sex toys. Yes, a person can have a favorite sex toy. Mine is a little suction cup vibrator that goes right over the clit. I dig through the suitcase looking for another velvet bag, one with a silicone dildo in it. Together, the two toys have given me some of the best orgasms I've had in the past two years.

Aside from last night.

THE SECRETS THAT WE KEEP 101

I slip the toys into the pockets of my robe and walk back into my room with a small smile. A smile that quickly fades when I see who's waiting on my bed. God, will this nightmare ever fucking end?

"What are you doing in here, Devon?" I sigh, rolling my eyes at him. His legs are stretched out and crossed at the ankles. He's made himself a nice looking little nest of pillows at his back.

"Well, when I called and you didn't answer, I was concerned." He holds my phone up with a smirk. The screen is cracked, a spider web shape spreading across the surface. "The only option I had was to come check on you myself."

"Riiight," I drawl, pulling the hem of my robe closer to my body.

"You know, I did miss you all these years." Devon kicks his legs over the edge of the bed, his big boots firm on the hard ground.

"Liar. You're too broken to miss anything but your own soul," I laugh as he walks toward me, his blue eyes holding me where I stand. I can't help but go back to that moment earlier today, when all I could think about was Devon and his sad blue eyes. How they reflect all the emptiness I feel. Emptiness that fades whenever he's near, or when his brother or Tate are with me.

He's in front of me now, his arm snaking around my waist, pulling me to him. Our noses practically touch as the tip of his moves along the side of my cheek, caressing my face with the sliver of air left between us.

"Oh, Rhyann. Nothing about me is broken." He pushes his groin into me. The hard ridge of his cock is all I can feel.

We stand for a minute, forehead to forehead. His mouth is so close I can almost taste the Sierra Nevada he was likely nursing before he came over. If I stick my tongue out, I'd likely taste the malty liquid on his lips. Fuck. My tongue aches to find out if I'm right.

I don't take my eyes off him, though. I won't be the one to back down. I'm standing on my toes to reach even a little bit of the height he has over me. It's impossible, but I try.

His hand caresses the small of my back, moving around to my hip. His fingers push past the slit in the side of my robe, where the deep pocket is. Where my dildo is.

In an effort to save myself utter humiliation, I turn away from his touch, pulling the side of my robe with me.

"Oh no you don't." Devon grabs onto my robe and pulls it back.

I have two choices. I can either let it fall open and continue my escape, or I can move with it, face the scrutiny of his icy gaze, and deal with the indignity of him knowing my only real intimate connections are with motorized, silicone encased hardware.

I choose the former. There are only two things that turn Devon Morris on. One is cruelty. No matter what he claims, someone broke him as a boy. The other, well, that's not my secret to tell. All I know is, seeing my naked body isn't going to do a goddamned thing for him.

I let my arms slide from the sleeves of the robe and flinch as the thud of my robe hitting the floor echoes in the room. God, I hope my vibrator didn't break. It should be fine, but I really like that one.

"Well, I'll be damned," Devon breathes out a gasp, my kernel of sadness over my vibrator turning to confusion.

One big hand sweeps around my waist, fingers wide and splayed across my flat belly. What the hell is he doing? I open my mouth to ask him but before a word passes my lips, I'm turned around and facing the most heartbreaking, exquisitely clear blue eyes I have ever seen.

"Not even my mother can tell us apart. But you," Devon sweeps a stray strand of hair. "How do you know, Rhyann? How have you always known?"

What the hell? What is he talking about? Anyone can see the differences between the brothers. Yes, they're identical, but at the same time they aren't. "I—I don't know. I just do. You're both so different."

The vitriol that usually hides in those blue eyes is gone, desperation taking its place. "But you prefer him, don't you?"

"I don't prefer either of you," I whisper, looking at the bright strands of red and gold and orange resting between Devon's fingers.

"No?" he asks, dropping my hair. "Do you think I wouldn't remember the drawing, Rhyann?"

Confusion etches across my face for a brief moment. Then I look down and it hits me. My tattoo! The dragonfly resting on a dandelion, with the wind swirling around its wings.

The picture Devon drew for me right before I was sent to Evangeline's. There were nights that sketch was the only thing keeping me going. I'd sit in my bed, in my dorm, and stare at it, wondering what Devon and Liam were doing. Was Tate with them? The drawing gave me hope for the summer.

Now, it's just a reminder of all the things that could have been. Wishes and whispers of secrets told in the dark. Hopes and dreams lost on the wind.

"Why?" Devon drops to his knees, running his fingers along the line work of the dragonfly body as it follows the length of my thigh. "Fucking perfect."

The brush of his lips over the blue ink is what turns my world upside down. It's so gentle, so—dare I say it—loving. His hands grip my thigh, firm and controlling but gentle and light as a feather.

"Devon, please," I beg.

He looks up at me, his nose nuzzling the spot where his lips had been. "Why did you get this?" he asks again, his grip on my thigh getting tighter.

"Be—" I swallow. My mouth is dry, my throat feels like sandpaper. I've never felt so exposed, so vulnerable as I do right here, right now. I'm standing naked in front of the one person who's ever made me forget myself, forget the pain and the loneliness. "Because it's always made me feel safe." I cry as tears form on my lashes.

"You mean, I make you feel safe?" the *I* is more a growl than a word.

"Please Devon," I beg, tears rolling down my cheeks like they were moments ago in the shower. "P—ple—"

My lips quiver, I can't get the word out before Devon scoops me up in his arms and claims my mouth with his. On instinct, my arms and legs wrap around Devon as he continues the onslaught.

My heart races in my chest, and my limbs shake. Of all the men in the world to come into my bedroom and literally sweep me off my feet with a kiss, Devon Morris is the last person I expected it to be.

I'm torn between begging him to stop and begging for more. My fingers dig into the collar of his shirt, nails scraping the flesh covering the taut muscles. My bare chest heaves against his and my nostrils fill with the spicy scents of cinnamon and cedar. I fight to catch my breath. I need to clear my head and stop this insanity before it consumes us both.

Devon lifts his leg and I can feel the soft dip as he kneels on my bed. Without breaking the kiss, he lays me down on the faux fur-lined duvet. My hands slide down his shoulders. Taking advantage of the shift in weight, I push at his chest, breaking the magnetic pull between us.

"Devon, stop," I say, breathy and low. "Why are you doing this?"

THE SECRETS THAT WE KEEP   107

His fingers caress down the side of my face, then my neck and shoulder. His hand quietly roams my bare flesh until he finds the tattoo on my hip once again. "I know your deepest secrets, Rhyann," he whispers. "I know who you think about at night when you touch yourself." His lips curl into a dark smile.

Devon reaches behind his back and pulls my tie-dyed, anatomically shaped dildo from his back pocket with a low laugh. "But my dick isn't multi-colored. And I'm pretty sure Tate's and Liam's aren't either."

"I fucking hate you," I spit. I should have seen this coming. He's hated me ever since he told me his secret. Everything Devon says or does is to hurt me, hurt people when their guard is down. Hot, angry tears threaten to spill over my lashes.

"Maybe. But you hate that I'm right, and you hate how your body responds to mine. I know you're wet." He kisses my cheek and slides his hand between my tightly closed thighs. He isn't wrong. I'm so fucking wet for him and I hate myself for it. I hate that I want it, I want him, and I wouldn't stop him if he tried to fuck me right here, right now.

"I hate myself," I confess, tears streaming down my cheeks. I turn my head in a fruitless attempt to hide them.

Not like it matters. I'm laying on my bed, as naked as the day I was born. Not to mention the sex toy that's now haphazardly laying at my side.

"Now, we have Tate's engagement party to go to." Devon stands up, and I can see the outline of his huge erection through his black pants. I look down at my dildo. That thing is nothing compared to the beast that's lurking between Devon's legs.

He knows it too, and based on the gloating smirk on his face, he knows I know it.

What the hell is wrong with me, wrong with these men? First, Liam cradles me to sleep the other night. I refuse to let my mind wander to what happened last night with Tate in my kitchen, and now this. With fucking Devon Morris!

"I don't want to go," I pout, no fucks left to give at this point.

"Oh, you're going. Tate fucking needs you there." His voice is barely above a whisper. "I need you."

"You should tell him before he marries this girl," I call as Devon turns his back on me to leave.

He doesn't look at me, he just stops at the door, his back straight. He knows what I'm talking about. "Wear something sexy. We're both going to need the distraction tonight."

"I told you, I don't want to go," I argue while I still can.

He sighs. "Stop lying to yourself, Rhy. You want to go, you know you need it as much as I do." He doesn't say anything else to me, just reaches for the door and steps out.

My fingers wrap around the silicone cock and I throw it as hard as I can at his head, but he's already closed the door behind him, and it hits the oak frame and falls to the ground.

Quagmire. I hate that word—such an asinine term, in my opinion. But this is more than a problem or predicament. It isn't a dilemma either. All those terms indicate solutions. No, there's no getting out of this noxious wet mess I've found myself in.

Chapter 9

Rhyann

The last thing I want to do right now is go to Tate's engagement party. I wasn't even invited! I throw one of the frilly decorative pillows in the same direction I threw the dildo.

Adrian had so many opportunities to invite me today, and he didn't mention it once. So why the hell would I want to tag along with Devon? A sharp pain stabs at my heart. Why wouldn't they invite me?

I sit up from the bed, furious, sexually frustrated, and emotionally exhausted. Out of the corner of my eye, I catch a flash of movement through the glass of the French doors that lead to the bedroom's private balcony. All my previous emotions are quickly washed away by a wave of panic.

My head snaps to the double doors. The face looking back at me is a frightening sight. It isn't any person. Well, not a stranger at least, but certainly not human. I frown at my reflection as it stares back at me from the glass. My red hair a chaotic mess of spun fire, my green eyes red rimmed and swollen from spending the better part of an hour crying. Either by myself in the shower, or on my bed.

Why the hell would Devon want to take me to any party is beyond me. With a sigh, I pick up the clothes I dropped on the floor when I found Dev sitting on my bed and get dressed. No, I'm not wearing anything sexy. No, I'm not doing my makeup and hair. And no, I'm definitely not going to any engagement party that I was intentionally not invited to.

I grab my phone, which is surprisingly not broken, off my bed and walk out into the empty hall. I get to the edge of landing at the top of the stairs and look over the balcony into the large foyer at the man waiting patiently below. His blonde hair is cut much shorter than his twin's, and his broad shoulders and muscular chest could be sculpted from marble. His long, strong legs are crossed at the ankles. He's dressed all in black, from head to toe. The black t-shirt hugs every line and curve, accentuates every muscle it covers. Paired with the black cargo pants and black boots, he looks as menacing as I know him to be.

He's so engrossed in his phone, he doesn't seem to notice me standing here watching him. What I wouldn't give to go down there and demand that we finish what we started in my room, that he relieve the tension and ease the numbness inside me. But I won't. Even if I did, he'd laugh. He loved teasing me as a kid, and when we got older and I'd come home to visit, the teasing evolved into disdain. Whatever that was in my room, he did it to hurt me in some way. I just can't figure out what.

I return to my room and lock the door before I send Devon the text letting him know I'm not feeling well, and am going to bed early.

Within seconds of hitting send on my phone, there's knocking on the door.

"Go away Dev. I told you, I'm tired," I say, holding back angry tears.

"No. You told him you're not feeling well," a voice that certainly is not Devon's says in response.

Fucking hell. Why is Liam here now too? With a frustrated sigh, I open my door. Liam is standing next to his brother wearing the biggest, brightest smile. It's a stark contrast to the scowl Devon wears as he looks me up and down.

"We don't have time for this shit, princess. Why aren't you ready?" Devon growls.

I roll my eyes. "I'm not going," I sigh. "I wasn't even invited."

"Sure you were!" Liam exclaims, his smile stretching across his face.

"I saw Adrian, and spoke to him twice today. He didn't mention it once." I start to close my door. "I'm not in the mood to crash his son's party."

Just as the door's about to close on the twins, thick fingers grip the edge and push the door in my direction.

"That's because Adrian doesn't know about it," Devon explains. "Now, stop being a fucking baby, and get ready."

Liam's arm swings and connects with Devon's abdomen with a reverberating thwack. "What he means, Rhy, is that we can't have this party without you. It's the four of us against the world. Remember?"

Us against the world. I sigh. Both brothers watch me with a distant, sorrowful gaze. I know where their thoughts are right now. Mine are in the same place.

I nod my head silently and turn to change my clothes. My thoughts are in a far off place from another time. A time when five young children made promises to always have each other's backs. Man, did we fuck up that promise.

It's been a while since I've gone out. I wasn't a complete hermit and outcast in college; I did enjoy dressing up and going out. Liam said Adrian didn't know about this party, so I can't help but wonder if he's even going to be there. "Us Against The World" by Killswitch Engage blasts through my house, and I can't help but smirk. Tonight is going to be anything but the typical socialite engagement party.

I choose black, distressed denim shorts that are open at the sides and held together with black leather laces. I pair the shorts with a backless, corset-style halter top that laces shut in the front and a pair of thigh high black boots. Everything shows off the tattoos I've gotten over the years. There aren't many and my dragonfly is the biggest one, but they're all significant and have meaning.

I straighten my hair and leave it down and apply a black smokey eye look for my makeup. My lips are a deep burgundy lined in black to give a vampish look. Looking in the mirror one more time, I'm quite proud of what I see.

It's been a long time since I've seen the guys outside of a funeral home or talking to detectives about kidnappings, and I realize they don't really know me anymore, not the adult version of me. I don't know them either. With a deep breath and one last glance in the mirror, I decide to let my walls down tonight. I'm going to trust these assholes who also, for better or for worse, are my best friends.

This time, when I approach the landing at the top of the stairs, two sets of aquamarine eyes stare up at me. Devon lets out a low whistle and Liam, as always, is all smiles while he watches me descend the stairs.

"Well," Devon clears his throat. "I guess I did tell you to wear something sexy."

"I see you've gotten more ink since the last time I saw you." Liam nods, acknowledging the barely visible tattoo between my breasts and the dandelion and dragonfly peeking out through the spaces on my shorts.

I don't miss the noxious glare Devon gives his brother. "It's time to go. We're already late."

"What do you mean, late?" I ask, suddenly feeling insecure.

"Well, our little argument, then your tantrum over the old man not telling you about a party he wasn't invited to, put us behind," Devon explains with absolutely zero emotion.

An argument? I quirk a brow in his direction. Is that what he wants to call it? I walk down the stairs slowly. "Is that what that was earlier, an argument?" I smirk and brush past him.

I can feel the ice blue of his stare bore into my bare back as I walk away. There's no way he can miss the flames of my newest piece of art.

Chapter 10

Rhyann

It wasn't until we left the sanctuary of the estate that anticipation and worry began to wash over me. I grip Donna's steering wheel, slowing my breath and my heart rate. I'm second guessing my decision to go to this party when I pull into the underground parking garage.

The club most certainly is not a place I can see Adrian showing up at. It's gritty, industrial, loud, and dark. The club is inside an old warehouse that's been renovated to be the next up-and-coming hot spot in the city. It's the kind of place you know about because you know someone who knows someone who's been here before. It's not exclusive; you don't need special connections to get in. It's just one of those places that isn't well known enough to be trendy yet.

Liam parks his Jeep next to Donna and the brothers wait for me to get out. With a brother on each arm, the three of us make our way to the elevator that'll take us right up to the club.

The elevator in the garage dings, and the metal doors slide open. The black, brushed metal panels that make up the three walls frame beautiful beveled mirrors with ivy and roses etched into them. I press the button with the scrolling number twenty-three, the only one lit up, watch the doors close. They are the same brushed metal as the walls without the beautifully etched mirrors. Looking at the outside of the building, you'd never expect such an extravagantly detailed elevator, or the breathtaking nightclub it opens up to.

The elevator starts to move, and the red dotted letter on the screen above the door changes from 'B' to 'L' and continues to count upward. A ding reverberates through the small space, alerting us to each new level we pass. My fingers grip the small black purse slung over my shoulder.

The heady scents of cinnamon, sage, and citrus fill the air. I try to hold back the nervous moan that dances on my tongue. My clit throbs in its hooded nest of flesh. My hormones have never been as out of control as they are right now. The image of me pushing that red stop button and getting on my knees to beg for a twin sandwich heats my face.

THE SECRETS THAT WE KEEP 119

I suck my lip between my teeth. This is foreign territory for me. I haven't been alone with the Morris twins in years. Back then, they were just Tate's best friends and Gemma's mean brothers who liked to tease me when they didn't think anyone else was paying attention.

"What's the matter, princess? Afraid to be alone with us?" Devon gives me a devious grin, then looks over my head to his twin. As kids, they'd play these head games with me. Like they shared some secret, unspoken language that only the two of them knew. Gemma wasn't even privy to their secrets. I asked her a few times what it was all about. She would just shrug her shoulders and tell me she thought it had to do with them being identical twins. As she put it, they shared a creepy psychic twin bond.

"If you two are going to play your twin bullshit tonight, I'm just going to go back home," I warn them both.

"I have no idea what you're talking about," Liam laughs as he smiles past me at his brother.

"You're doing it now, and you know it." My voice lowers. My slender fingers reach out for the button panel.

Long, thick fingers wrap around my small bicep. "Don't even think about pressing any buttons."

I look up into Devon's icy blue eyes, and they're anything but cold. There's an unexpected fire behind them. The same fire that was there when he kissed me on my bed a couple hours ago.

"Not unless you plan on stopping the elevator," Liam's playful voice adds to the moment.

What in the ever loving fuck? Okay, I can rationalize the whole psychic twin shit, but seriously. I was just pushing the very inappropriate idea of a threesome with them from my thoughts.

"I—" Clearing my throat, I drop my hand and rest against the side of the elevator.

The ride up seems to drag on forever. This has got to be the slowest, quietest ride I've ever endured.

"I'm sorry." Devon's hypnotic baritone rings out through the silence, sending a chill down my spine. What the hell is wrong with me? This is Devon, Tate's best friend, Liam's brother. This is the same Devon that told Tate I had a crush on him when I was ten. He wasn't lying. I did have a huge crush on Tate. But I had a crush on Liam and Devon, too.

"Sorry for what?" I ask, afraid of what he's going to say.

"Sorry we weren't there to keep you safe before." He doesn't look at me. I know he's talking about the failed snatch and grab, the kidnapping that never happened.

"If something had happened to you..." Liam adds. He doesn't finish the sentence, though. The anger radiating off his and his brother's body is enough to tell me how they feel.

I forgot how to speak, how to respond to this dark admonition. When I graduated a few days ago, I swore to myself I wouldn't get tangled up in other people's emotions, that I would steer clear of any sentimental attachment, and I would focus on my career. But, here I am, in an elevator on my way up to a nightclub in the middle of an abandoned skyscraper in the city, with two men who I could never say no to.

"It's not a big deal," I sigh, finding the words to speak. "I'm here now. I'm safe, and I agreed to let your company handle my security."

I refuse to look at either brother. The fact that they're taking what happened so hard is another cold reminder of the one person who should be here with us. The one person all four of us miss more than anything. Gemma.

I always thought Tate would fall in love with and marry Gemma someday. I hoped for it, but at the same time I cried over the idea. Tate was like a dark fairytale prince when we were kids. He was always just barely out of reach, there but not really. He was cruel and kind in the same breath. Gentle and rough with the same two hands. I loved him and I hated him all at once, but he always protected me from others, even the twins. Unless it was all a part of whatever game Tate was playing, the twins treated me like a precious gem to be cherished.

That first summer I came home after Gemma's death, all three of the guys were in dark places. They spent the entire summer at my grandfather's house, brooding and watching me. I wasn't allowed to go out with any of the local kids my age, not without an escort. Every phone call, every text I got, if one of them were around, they took my phone and responded for me. Without my consent, of course.

I roll my eyes, thinking about how controlling they were until they disappeared from my life. For nearly six years.

"Look at me." Dev's fingers dig into muscle—I didn't realize he was still holding onto me— and he pulls me to him. My mind fights it, but my feet obey like the pathetic things they are.

I have to crane my neck to look him in the eyes. He towers over my five foot two with his whopping six foot six. Gone was the lanky, tall, Jack Skellington-like teenage boy. I stare up at the beast of a man whose glowing eyes haunt most women's fantasies.

"H-hi." I stutter like a little girl facing her hero. But he's no hero. Not to me, at least. He's the villain. The boogeyman under my bed and in my closet.

"Are you afraid of me, Rhyann?" Devon picks up a strand of my hair, wrapping it around one of his fingers, his eyes not once leaving mine.

"No," I whisper. I'm not afraid of him. I'm afraid of me, and the way my body reacts to him.

"You know, I always like it when you're afraid. Your skin gets this rosy pink flush, and your eyes turn to a dark green. Just like right now."

"I'm not afraid of you, Devon." I straighten my shoulders, pulling my arm from his grip. "You guys need to find a new hobby. I'm too old for your bullshit games."

I muster the strength to turn away and face the front of the elevator once more. The light above the door flashes from twelve to thirteen. I groan. Ten more floors in this cramped moving box. Wonderful.

Devon grabs me by the arm again. This time, he turns and pushes me against the back wall, his big hands resting on the brass rails in front of the mirrored walls. "You're right, princess. You're not a little girl anymore." Devon's words come out in a growl. I look at Liam and he just shrugs. His own blue eyes are hooded and dark.

My breath catches in my throat. "Knock it off, Devon."

"Or what?" he asks.

I pull the inside of my cheek between my molars. I really have nothing. I'm so small compared to Devon, even though we fit together like two pieces of a puzzle. Well, three pieces, because I can't look at Devon without needing Liam, and vice versa.

I look past Devon to his brother, who watches us intensely. His arms are tightly crossed over his chest. With a moan, I look back at Devon, thoughts of him holding me in place while Liam runs his tongue down my neck to the valley between my breasts shooting through my brain.

Fuck, what's wrong with me? Why do I keep thinking about having sex with both of them? It must be the shock of everything I've been through this week. I don't feel like I'm in shock; I don't feel overly anxious or nervous, at least not when the guys are with me.

"Well, princess. What are you going to do?" Devon's voice snaps me out of my thoughts. I open my mouth to speak. What I'm going to say, I don't know, but I need to say something.

"We're here," Liam announces. His voice cuts through the tension in the elevator moments before the bell dings and the small cab comes to a jolting stop.

The metal doors open to a simple, elegant restaurant. Red carpeting stretches from wall to wall. The oak paneled half walls on either side of us feature the same scrolling designs as the elevator we just left. There are men and women in varying degrees of dress, but all of them are in finer clothes. This is definitely not the place for the clothing I wore.

Turning to my left, I glare at Liam. "You could have told me to change," I seethe. Liam had always been just a little bit kinder, warning me when he could of Devon's childish pranks.

"I could have. But then you would have changed out of this." He nods his head as he looks me over.

"Trust me princess, you're dressed to perfection," Devon whispers in my ear, and I fight the urge to elbow him in his ribs.

Standing on either side of me, both men take my arms in theirs and we walk up to the hostess like we own the place.

"Good evening, gentleman," the hostess greets us. "Table for three?"

"We'll be having one more join us shortly," Liam says energetically.

"Of course," the woman smiles.

She is beautiful. Her long, straight black hair shines and frames her face perfectly as it cascades down to rest above full breasts that are nearly spilling out from the top of her tight white blouse. Her long slender legs peek out of a half length black pencil skirt, and the patent leather black heels make the perfect dot at the bottom of her human exclamation point. I do my best to hide the scowl on my face.

She seats us at a small round table in the far corner of the restaurant. Flameless candles sit in clear glasses in the center of the table and wrought iron, electric sconces line the walls behind us. This is not the club I was expecting to go to, but I do like it. It gives a 1930s glam vibe.

THE SECRETS THAT WE KEEP   127

"I thought we were going to a club, not a restaurant," I hiss after the hostess leaves us with menus and slowly sashays back to her station.

"Calm down princess." The way Devon calls me princess is condescending and laced with vitriol. It's a complete one-eighty from the adoration in his tone hours ago.

"Fuck you, Devon. I'm not doing this shit." I push my chair back and stand up. They told me this was a night-club. It feels like there's a swarm of bees flying around in my stomach.

As if it were rehearsed, both brothers reach out and grasp my arms in unison. Liam's touch is feather soft and gentle. Devon's is possessive, tight, and commanding. His fingers press into my pulse point as he glares up at me.

"Sit your pretty little ass down and do something you've never done before," he growls, so low only Liam and I can hear.

I pull my arm from Liam's grip, but when I go to do the same with the wrist Devon holds, his fingers tighten around me.

"Rhy, don't make a scene," Liam cautions.

It's just like him, taking his brother's side. Every fucking time. Sure, he would do what he could to protect me, but in the end, he'd always choose to appease Devon.

"I'm..." I bend forward, staring into the icy blue of Devon's eyes, my tits on perfect, beautiful display, taunting him and Liam, "...leaving," I say slowly, waiting for each word to sink in.

"If you don't sit your ass down, princess—"

"What are you gonna do?" I laugh. Devon's never done anything to hurt me, not in public, not physically. He doesn't scare me. Tate's always held a tight leash on his two best friends where I'm concerned. But Tate's getting married. To some woman I didn't even know he was seeing.

If I'm being honest with myself, I don't really know Tate at all. I don't know Devon or Liam. Not the men they've become, not who they are now. I know the boys who used to tease me when their sister and Tate weren't around. They were the boys who I dreamed of marrying one day, living together in my grandfather's big house. I know the first kiss, the first heartbreak, and the shared childhood fears and nightmares. I don't know the men they've become, or what made Devon so empty and cold. I know the summer spent with Liam when my grandfa-

THE SECRETS THAT WE KEEP   129

ther died, but I don't know the man he was before or after
I went back to school.

"If you don't sit down right now Rhyann," Devon uses
my name like a knife, slowly pushing it through the flesh
of my chest, the tip piercing my heart, "I'm going to put
you over my knee and spank you until you beg me to
stop."

He stands up, his eyes locked with mine. His hand is
still holding my wrist in its firm grip. I should be afraid. I
really should. But I'm not. If anything, I'm turned on by
his words. My hips shift and my clit brushes against the
seam of my shorts.

"You wouldn't," I breathe out with a groan. Oh god,
why didn't I wear underwear?

Devon runs a finger down the side of my face, wrapping his long fingers around my jaw, holding my gaze.
"Try me."

"Tate won't allow it," I whisper. "He's gonna be pissed
if he sees you holding me like this."

Liam laughs behind me. *Liam*! The sensible, reason-
able twin.

"Would he though?" Devon raises an eyebrow.

"Fuck you," I seethe, pulling my arm from Devon's
grip. This time, he lets me go, dropping both hands with

a smirk. He can see the tears welling up in my eyes as I fight them back. I won't cry over these dickheads.

I clear my throat and am about to grab my purse and leave when a server brings over a basket of warm bread and some herb-infused butter. "The ladies' room is down that hall and to the right," she says, pointing to a hallway across the dining room.

Do I look that fucking bad? "I was just leaving, anyway," I tell her.

"Oh. Well, I do hope you'll change your mind," she says awkwardly. "I'll come back for your drink orders."

As she walks away, I back away from the table, my purse in hand, and walk in the direction of the restroom. I fix my hair, my slightly smudged lip color, and blot the little streaks of black that started under my eyes. My hair is fine, bright fiery red tresses flowing down my bare back.

I take a deep breath, watching myself in the mirror. Despite nearly crying, I'm still turned on. I need to get out more, make some friends, find a boyfriend, a fuck buddy, something to stop me from acting like a thirsty bitch lost in the desert. I moan softly, shifting my hips so my clit rubs against the seam of my shorts again. I really should have worn underwear.

My fingers slide down past the waistband of my shorts and slide over the waxed smooth mound of my pubis until they find my swollen little bean. My other hand grips the edge of the counter as I massage light little circles over the cluster of nerves. Pressing deeper as my fingers continue their motion, my hips join in the dance, rocking ever so slightly, in sync with my fingers.

My legs shake as the pressure builds between my thighs. Memories of the night before and Tate's mouth over my clit floods my mind. I can still feel Devon's hand over my wrist. The same wrist that's currently working my clit. God, what would it be like to have the two of them together? I look at myself in the mirror, my cheeks pink, my lips glistening. I imagine the cool sky blue of Liam's gaze on me while his brother and best friend make me cum and that's all I need. My clit pulses under my fingers and I feel the first tiny wave of an orgasm hit. My thighs tremble as I press into my little bean, milking the orgasm from my body.

After a few minutes, I collect my thoughts. I push the strange fantasy of an orgy with my three friends aside. That's a topic for a therapy session that'll never happen. I take my time collecting myself. I wash my hands, make sure I didn't cum all over my shorts, or at least make sure it's not obvious I just made myself cum in the bathroom of some restaurant. Then I smooth my hair out and leave the quiet little bathroom with a smile.

"Took you long enough."

Before the sound of the voice behind me registers, I turn around, swinging my fist in the direction of Devon's face. Thanks to his lightning fast reflexes, he catches my wrist in his strong hands.

"Fucking hell!" I exclaim. I'm shaking in his hold as an invisible vice tightens around my chest.

"Hey. Rhyann," Devon's voice is soft but commanding. "Look at me."

I look up at him, my vision hazy through the tears that won't stop trying to escape my eyes. Swallowing the knot in my throat, I give him a weak smile. "Sorry," I whisper.

My emotions are making me dizzy. One minute, I hate him with a passion, the next I'm making myself cum from fantasies of him and his brother and Tate, and now I can't figure out if I want to fight him off me or run screaming.

"Rhyann," he sighs. "Fuck, you're shaking." Devon pulls my arm until I'm flush with his broad chest. His strong arms wrap around me, and warm, soft lips press firmly into the top of my head.

After a couple minutes of Devon's fingers roaming up and down my spine, I lift my head and look into his glacial blue eyes. I can see Liam doing this, comforting me, calming me down. But Devon? Never in a million years would I expect him, of all people, to be the one to chase away my fears.

"You've been through a lot," he starts. "I know you haven't processed what happened to you."

"I—" He cuts me off with his finger to my lips before I can argue.

"Don't deny it, Rhyann. I'm not as dumb as I act." Devon's hands move up my back and grip my shoulders, holding me in place. "You're stronger than most women, but you went through some trauma the other night. You can let it out later. Fuck, I'll let you take it out on me if you want. But right now, our best friend needs us both. So, will you please come back to the table, behave yourself, and try to have a good time?"

I nod my head with a sigh, earning me a devious smile from my companion.

"Good girl," he says, his voice laced with something dark and haughty. "But don't think you've gotten out of that spanking."

What. The. Fuck? I don't budge as he starts to pull me back to the table. To Liam, and the rest of the people dining in a fancy restaurant, looking polished and posh when I look like a high priced call girl.

Devon turns to me, his icy blue eyes staring deeply into my sea-green ones. His gaze is so intense, my clit aches all over again, needing more than a quick flicking in a public bathroom. A wicked smile spreads across his face as he lifts my hand to his mouth and brushes his perfect red lips across my knuckles and winks at me.

Chapter 11

Rhyann

As we walk back to our table, we both stop when we notice two new bodies seated there with Liam. Right away, Tate's tall, slender form is recognizable. His sandy blonde hair is freshly trimmed in the back and at the sides. Next to him, a head full of fluffy, shining, wavy white-blonde hair cascades over bare, sun kissed shoulders.

The hairs on the back of my neck bristle, and instantly I don't like her. I haven't even seen her face, and I already know she has a horse's face. Even if she really doesn't, in my mind, she absolutely does.

Liam notices our approach and smiles darkly in our direction. Tate and his companion turn to see what he's looking at, and the woman's light brown eyes light up. Tate's face, on the other hand, contorts into something that reflects a mix of pain, anger, and sadness all rolled into one ugly scowl.

All the awkwardness and desire to go home that I left in the hallway by the bathroom comes rushing back the second I lock eyes with Tate. He doesn't want me here, and he isn't hiding it.

"Don't," Devon whispers, digging his fingers into my side when I make the tiniest movement to turn around and hightail it out of here. "Don't give him what he wants, princess. He made his bed. He can fucking lay in it."

I straighten my back and lean closer into Devon's embrace as we make our way to the table. Devon's thumb caresses the bare skin above my hip, sending warm little jolts of electricity from the spot where his hand is to the core of my womanhood. I bite my lip to keep myself from moaning in front of all these well-to-do, respectable patrons.

"I thought you guys were bringing dates," Tate says, standing up and taking his best friend's hand in his. "Rhyann." He nods at me in greeting, avoiding any kind of physical contact.

Air hisses through my teeth, a knee jerk reaction to the absolute coldness directed at me. I'd expect that from Devon, or maybe—on a bad day—Liam, but never from Tate. Until now, he's always had my back, been my biggest support and best friend. Until now, until this...girl.

Think of the devil, and she shall appear. Goldilocks chooses this moment to focus her attention on me, a bright, perfect smile on her face, dimpling her round, naturally rosy cheeks.

"Hi," she says, bouncy and perky, embodying the definition of femininity. Her soft voice barely rises over the muted chatter of the busy restaurant. She extends her left hand to me. A gleaming solitaire diamond the width of her finger winks at me. "I'm Aubree. You must be Devon's date."

I take her hand hesitantly. Bitch is catty. I have to respect how she subtly marked her territory immediately by flashing the gigantic rock in all our faces.

"Rhyann." I smile at her. She wants a pissing contest, I'll give her one. "And, yes, I'm Devon's date. Liam's too."

Liam laughs, giving me a wink. Devon's grip around my waist tightens and I smirk up at him. A low growl comes from Tate's direction.

"Oh. Well, it's nice to meet you, Rhyann."

The two of us sit down in our designated chairs. Aubree is beside Tate, closest to the corner of the room and away from either of the twins. My seat is pleasantly nestled between the twins, directly across from Tate, who looks like someone just shit all over his prime rib.

Tate settles into his own chair, his intense silver gaze bouncing angrily from Devon to Liam and back. I laugh softly as he makes an obvious point to avoid me at all costs.

"So, Aubree," I break the silence with a cheerful tone. "How did you and Tate meet?"

Aubree, who's been sitting in her little corner sulking over the discomfort in the air, perks up and smiles brightly in my direction.

"Oh. Our fathers are business associates," she beams. "We met a year ago at a charity event his father's company put on."

"Oh, you mean..." I smile as brightly as I can. Looking in Liam's direction, he finds it as amusing as I do—she has no idea who I am.

"Rhyann, please," Tate looks at me, an expression I can't put my finger on in his eyes.

"Devereux Publications?" I ask, holding in my sinister giggle. I don't know what petty, vindictive snake stuck its fangs in me and spread its poison throughout my veins, but I am going to enjoy this tonight.

"Yes," Aubree says, a radiant smile stretching across her cherubic face. "I didn't know you knew Adrian or his company."

"His company," I muse, giving Tate a smirk, my eyebrow cocked. I'm about to ask him to explain when the server from earlier returns to the table with an embossed wooden plaque in her hand.

"The drink menu." She holds the piece of wood out. "To get you started?"

"That won't be necessary," Liam says, looking at our party. "We will all be having a Sazerac."

"Oh. Well." The server's expression changes and she clears her throat. "It'll be just a few minutes, sir." She leaves the drink menu on the table, then walks away quickly, an excited sparkle in her eyes.

"What's a Sazerac?" Aubree asks as I pick up the drink menu, scanning it to give her an answer.

"Umm..." I look up at her in confusion. "It's not on the menu."

"Well, I don't want a drink that I don't know the ingredients of." I have to agree with her. I'm not in the mood for experimenting tonight.

"Don't worry," Devon whispers in my ear. "It's the code word."

My head snaps in his direction. With him on one side of me, and Liam on the other, I can see how some might get them confused. They have the same blue eyes, the same blonde hair, the same noses. But I see the differences. The way one of Liam's eyes squints just a little more than the other when he smiles, or Devon's shallow little dimples.

Code words, mysterious restaurants in the middle of an abandoned high rise, waiting for what seems like a lifetime without so much as a food menu. My eyes narrow as I stare at Devon, then look to Tate, who is looking anywhere but in my direction, and then Liam, who's watching me as intensely as Tate is avoiding me. The brothers both have a devious smile on their faces. One I know all too well, one that promises devilry is to come.

As if Liam can read my thoughts, he nods in confirmation. We are at a speakeasy. A new one from what I gathered based on the details the brothers gave me on the way here. I've never been to a speakeasy. I bite my lip to stifle the excited giggle working its way up my throat. Aubree continues to panic over someone ordering a drink she didn't ask for. Gasp! My eyes roll on their own as we watch the tantrum of a spoiled debutant unfold.

"Is this girl for real?" Liam leans back and asks his brother quietly.

Something familiar rattles around in the back of my mind.

"I'm afraid so," Devon laughs behind me. It's deep, dark, and warm.

"Wait, I thought you guys knew her already," I add, not taking my eyes from Tate as he tries to explain the situation to his fiancee.

Devon wraps his long fingers around the back of my neck, pulling my ear closer to his lips. "Do you really think if we had met the brat earlier, we would have let this happen?"

What? The guys hadn't met her until tonight? Interesting. Maybe the three of them haven't been as close as they used to be. "How long have they been dating?" I ask quietly.

"I think six months," Liam answers.

"She probably cried and stomped her feet and threw a tantrum just to get that first date," Devon whispers back.

The snort happens before I can stop it, and both Aubree and Tate look my way. I giggle and wave at

Aubree, ignoring Tate. Two can play this game, asshole. The near snarl I get in response from her has both me and Liam practically falling out of our chairs with laughter.

"See, I told you your friends wouldn't like me."

Devon clears his throat, his fingers tightening around the back of my neck. Liam and I glance at the couple across the table. Tate is tomato faced and I swear, if he were a cartoon, there'd be smoke coming out his ears. I'm trying so hard not to laugh when I look over at Aubree.

Her face is contorted into a clown-like frown. One of those "smile now cry later" clowns from the early nineties. Her doe-like brown eyes are squinted like she's forcing the tears to fall. I don't see any tears, though. Her perfectly applied makeup is intact, her face as dry as the finishing powder she applied before leaving her house today.

"Oh. No, honey," I say in the same tone I would use with an irrational child. "No one dislikes you."

"Yet," Liam says under his breath, for only me and Devon to hear. He's close enough that I jab my elbow into his side and get a muffled "oomph" as reward.

"Aubree. What do you do for work?" I ask, changing the subject. I had to deal with my fair share of spoiled rich brats at the boarding school, and these girls love nothing more than talking about themselves.

"Well, nothing yet." Her voice perks up and she smiles. The crocodile tears are suddenly gone. "But, daddy promised me that as soon as Tate and I are married, I can go to work for Adrian as his personal assistant."

I have never met someone so vapid and dense until now. Aubree looks proud of herself over her announcement, and her fiance is obviously uncomfortable. Good. He has some explaining to do. So does Adrian, and he said I'd like this girl. Ha!

"Oh. Well. The personal assistant to a CEO of a multimedia corporation, that's got to take a lot of schooling, right?"

"Well, a business degree would be useful," she informs me. Which, yes, she is correct. However, I will not be keeping her on as my personal assistant when I take over in a few months.

"Oh, you have your MBA?" I ask excitedly.

Aubree giggles, Tate bristles, and the twins are just sitting back, relaxed, watching this interaction unfold. "Oh god no. I didn't bother with college." The way she says the words seems like she is fighting to keep herself from vomiting all over the table.

"How do you expect to do the job, then?" I ask, confused, but not really. I know what her answer will be. "You said a business degree is useful."

"Useful, but unnecessary. A trained monkey can do the job," she smirks.

I'm about to say something, or maybe even reach across the table and slap the self righteous look on this bitch's face, when Tate stands up and clears his throat. "Aubree, love. Why don't you go to the ladies' room and freshen up? I'm sure we'll be moving on to another room shortly."

"I'll go with her," I say, a little too enthusiastically.

"No, I'll walk her there myself." Tate growls in my direction. "Dev, a word with my best man, please?"

The look Tate gives me is one of absolute disgust. It's as though the past twenty-four years of my existence was nothing more than a bad dream he'd like to forget. It's obvious Tate doesn't want me here. I'm not sure what I did to make him hate me so much between what he did last night in my kitchen and now.

I came tonight thinking I'd get answers, that Tate would be the same Tate he'd been my entire life. The same boy who would tease me about my red hair, but turn around and punch his best friend in the gut for doing the same thing. The same Tate who climbed into bed with me and held me when I cried in the dark after I found my father dead, hanging from his office ceiling, when I was ten years old.

No, the Tate I'm watching walk away now is someone unfamiliar to me. Someone I've never met before. The Tate I knew would never have put up with spoiled little rich brats like Aubree. Again, something familiar rattles around in the back of my mind as I watch her blonde curls bounce over her shoulders as she walks away from the table. Her sleeveless yellow sundress swishes around her legs as she walks.

Who wears a sundress out at night in the Bay Area? Sure, it's late May, and California, but it's still the bay! It's wet and cool at night. The fog rolls in from the ocean, making the fifty-three degree weather feel like thirty-three degrees. But who am I to question her clothing choices when I'm wearing practically nothing myself.

"Now I see why he's in a shit mood whenever he comes back from visiting with her." Liam pulls me from my thoughts on the weather.

"What do you mean?"

He sits forward, and his scent of citrus and sage fills my nostrils and relaxes me. In some way, Liam has always been calming. Just his presence smoothes whatever edges I feel forming. "Well, he's been going back and forth between here and Seattle for months to see her, and every time he comes home, he's in a shit mood for days."

Interesting. "It's obvious he doesn't want me here, Liam," I confess.

"We know." Liam looks down at his hands. He's dressed in black from head to toe. Black suede and canvas tactical boots, black cargo pants, and a black long sleeve shirt. Sensible.

"What do you mean, 'we know'?" I ask, staring at him.

"When Dev told him we were picking you up, Tate said to leave you home."

I try not to flinch as his confession cuts at my soul. "Why am I here then?"

"Because you're a part of the group. You're one of us," Liam says with a soft smile. "Just because Tate forgot that little bit doesn't mean Devon and I have."

Chapter 12

Rhyann

After the guys return to the table with Aubree, we're led down a hall to a door labeled Employees Only. On the other side of the door is a stairwell. It looks like the emergency exit route, or what used to be. The white plastered walls are covered in movie posters from different eras in Hollywood history.

The metal staircase is covered in steel diamond plate. While it's obvious the restaurant has been updated, the stairwell has not. There are worn spots where the raised pattern in the flooring has been walked over countless times by who knows how many people. Even the lighting is outdated. The overhead lights buzz and flicker every few minutes.

"Where are we going?" Aubree asks, breaking the monotony of silence that's engulfed us all.

"We're going to a speakeasy," I explain. Tate hasn't said a word to me since he came back from the restrooms. He hasn't spoken to anyone to be precise.

"I've never been to a speakeasy." I look over at Aubree, her big brown doe eyes bright with excitement.

The club, aptly called The Dive, is on the floor below the restaurant. It's a mix of 1920s glam with a metalcore slash industrial chaser. Now I see why the codeword was a prohibition-era drink. Not just because it's a speakeasy, but also because the entire place is a modernized interpretation of the aesthetic of the time. The club takes up several floors of the building. The center is hollowed out to reveal a large dance floor at the heart of it all. Each floor is slightly different, but all staying within the scope of the theme.

The first floor, the one we came in at, acts as a lobby of sorts. It's the most brightly lit area of the place. Wood panels along the walls, plush carpeting that matches the restaurant above. There are even lacquered wood tables and red velvet arm chairs scattered throughout the space.

"Rhyann, look," Aubree gasps, grabbing my arm.

When I look in the direction her fingers are pointing, I see a couple servers dressed all in red, with sheer black hose covering their legs, and black kitten heels. The servers are carrying boxes attached to straps slung around their necks. Cigarette girls.

"Isn't that cute?" Aubree asks. "Even their staff is dressed to play the part. I wonder if there are any flappers."

"I don't know, maybe," I say, taking in our surroundings. This floor has a wood panel railing to keep people from inadvertently falling to their deaths because they're too drunk or too dumb to pay attention to the ledge.

"Why don't we find a quiet seat and order something to eat?" Tate finally speaks up.

An excited tingle courses through my veins. I look up thinking he's talking to the group, to me. But he's looking at Aubree, his back to me and the twins. Of course. I sigh and return to scanning the club. Looking at the different floors, I can see how each one differs. The closer you get to the last level, the beating heart of the club, the main dance floor, the levels change slightly; they become darker, less plush, and more industrial.

"Guys," I hear Tate say. "You coming?"

When I look back at my friend, he's already turned his back to me and is guiding his fiancee to a discreet table in the corner. I look at Devon, who is following silently behind Tate. He hasn't said a word to me since they came back, either.

Liam rests his hand on my shoulder. "Come on, Rhy. Let's eat something before we have a little fun."

"I'll meet you there. Order something for me," I tell him.

"What are you up to?" he asks with a smirk.

"Nothing," I assure him. "I'm going to go find the ladies' room."

He nods and lets me go. "Don't take too long. The three of us are already on Tate's shit list."

I laugh as I watch Liam follow his brother and best friend. Tate's shit list. Well, who made him the president of this little club? Oh yeah, he did. Well, fuck that! I'm a grown ass woman, I can do whatever I want. Besides, he doesn't want me here. So why the hell should I return to a group where I'm not welcome?

I find the restrooms down a short hallway near the stairs leading to the other floors. The ladies' room is as posh as I expected it to be. Gilded wallpaper stretches from corner to corner, with soft black carpeting throughout the main part of the room. There are four cherry wood doors with gold handles across the far wall.

When a woman walks out of one, I catch sight of a regular-looking toilet on the tile floor.

The sinks are shaped like clam shells and painted in the style of Greek fresco artwork. There are even tufted, velvet stools in front of brightly lit vanity tables for women to fix their makeup or hair during the night. It's all well thought out and beautiful. It's not just a secret nightclub, it's an experience. It's a throwback to a time that no one alive today has lived through, and whoever had this vision, they did it well.

I smooth my hair, make sure no traitorous tears escaped my lashes earlier, and leave the restroom. On one side of me is a carpeted staircase leading to the floor below. On the other side is the lobby where the guys are waiting for me. But are they really? I'm sure Tate is relieved I disappeared.

My curiosity gets the better of me and I make my way down the stairs. The second floor down is slightly darker than the one above. A black satin curtain, held open by leather straps, separates the stairway from the rest of the floor. Rather than red textiles strewn throughout the room, there are black velvet chairs at the tables and black carpeting under my feet.

The portraits on the walls depict a more burlesque style. Paintings of nude women with fans made of feathers covering their naughty bits. The servers weaving their way between the tables look the same as the ones from the floor above with one exception. They ditched the cigarette caddies and are instead pushing metal drink carts. I find the stairway to the next floor, this one another darker version of the one I just came from.

At the end of the stairs, I don't find another curtain. There's a black wooden door, no knob, but there's a small wrought iron cage covering a panel in the door. I go out on a limb and knock on the door.

The small panel swings open and I'm met with a set of dark eyes, a sharp nose, and a mouth framed by a thick black beard. "Password?" he asks simply.

I give it a thought for a second. I hadn't expected a second password would be needed. "Sazerac?" I ask, taking a chance.

The person behind the door closes the panel, which is actually called a speakeasy. That's where the term derived from. Ordinary businesses would front for bootlegged bars. They'd have secret doors with sliding panels in them for people to see and speak through.

I turn around, my shoulders slumped in defeat, and begin to ascend the stairs when the door opens behind me. I stifle a giggle and turn on my heel, rushing through the private door before the bouncer behind it changes his mind and shuts me out.

This floor is different from the two above it. It's edgier than the others. Gone is the carpeting, and in its place is hardwood that's worn and lost the luster and shine of new flooring. It has to be intentional; the rough hewn wood adds to the ambience of the floor. The velvet chairs are gone too, dark brown leather replacing them at the large wooden tables. The railing that's open to the floor below, the last level of this riveting new club, has lost most of the wooden panels along the half wall, making it more open.

I make my way to the railing, hoping for a better look at the floor below me. I'm close to the dance floor now, and can actually feel the music coming from the speakers beneath my feet.

My heart races as I catch my breath. So many people, so many bodies crowded together, grinding against each other in varying levels of dress. I am elated over my choice of clothing now. I've never been much of a party girl, never really cared to go out and be in huge crowds, but the adrenaline coursing through me at this moment has clouded my judgment.

I turn quickly, looking for the staircase leading to the last floor. It's not that hard to find. It's on the same side of the room that the first one was in. The floor plan for each level seems to mirror the one above it. Simple and easy to remember. In true form, this set of stairs compliments both floors it connects.

With each step, the corridor gets darker, the lights dimmer, and the music louder. I stop dead in my tracks at the bottom step and suck in a breath. This time there's no door blocking me from my destination, no satin or velvet curtain either. Just a sheet of shimmering metal. Small silver chain link strands cascade down the mouth of the stairway, glittering against the darkness I descended from.

My hand reaches out, touching the cool, delicate metal. I run my fingers down a few strands, letting the anticipation build inside me before I cross the threshold. If I do this, there's no going back. Nothing will be the same. Maybe that's what I need. What if this is me breaking from my shell, from the chains I allowed myself to be shackled in all these years.

THE SECRETS THAT WE KEEP

My friends have moved on. Tate's engaged and wants to forget about me. Fine. I can do that too. I can't make sense of the strange tension between me, Devon, and Liam. That's fine too. I don't want to right now, anyway. This moment, this club, this is my chance to find myself, my world, and explore it.

My fingers wrap around a length of chain, ready to take the step into the unknown. Rough hands wrap around mine and I'm pulled into the arms of a stranger. Hazy memories of the other night flood my brain. Blinded and restrained, being forced into the dirty trunk of a car. My fight-or-flight response kicks in and I swing at the person who ripped me from the safety of the stairs.

"Hey, hey. I won't bite," a soft male voice whispers gently. "I promise."

I wait for the stale booze and swamp ass smell to overwhelm me. But it never comes. I look up as the intoxicating scent of the redwoods and leather fills my nostrils.

"Hi," I breathe out.

"Hello there," the stranger laughs, still holding my hand. "You look lost."

"Well, I'm not." I bristle, yanking my hand free of his grasp.

His scent fills up my space again. I look up at the face of the man in front of me to find pitch black eyes staring at me from a face full of hard edges. The only part of his face that isn't sharp is the mirthful smile he's wearing. There's a knot on the bridge of his nose, pushing it slightly to one side. A tell-tale sign of someone who's had their nose broken a time or two. Jet black tendrils of hair curl around the shape of his ear and spill down his forehead.

He's not bad to look at, I'll give him that much. But something about the encounter isn't sitting well with me, and my skin bristles when he speaks again.

"My name's Cole. You are?" he asks huskily.

I brush the ominous feeling off as an aftereffect of the forced flashback from the botched kidnapping and smile up at him. "Rhyann," I say with a smile.

"Well, Rhyann, can I buy you a drink?" Cole asks.

I can barely hear him over the pulsing beat of the music. I turn my gaze to the dance floor, my foot tapping to the rhythm of the music playing. The lights above are flashing and moving in varying shades of neon. That's what I came down here for. The heart of the club, the music, the life blood beating and coursing through the veins of the building, bringing it to life.

I've completely tuned out everything around me, including Cole, and head straight for the dance floor. "Judas" by Banks is calling to me like a siren's song, luring me to join the denizens as they sweat and grind up against each other. Pushing my way through the throng of bodies, I find my place on the bacchian altar. I'm neither surprised nor irritated to find that Cole followed me into the center of the crowd. I begin to dance as the song winds down and the next one picks up.

We dance together through the next three songs. Tate and Aubree are forgotten in the haze of music and light and perspiration. Liam and Devon and their world of mixed signals are pushed to the darkest parts of my mind. For a moment, I start to forget about my new companion as I give myself over to the music. My body is an offering to Bacchus as the world around me dissolves, and all that's left is me, the music, and the lights.

As "Obscene" by Marilyn Manson ends, the crowd is hyped up and jumping along with the beat. I turn to Cole and smile, pushing my way out of the crowd to the bar. The back wall of this floor is lined in corrugated steel, and metal panels hide the lighting along the wall, giving the metal a glowing effect.

I ask for a bottle of water and Cole grabs my wrist before I can take it from the bartender.

"Let me buy you a drink," he says.

I accept the water and smile at the man beside me. I know better than to let a stranger buy me a drink at the bar. Even if I do watch them order the drink and it's handed directly to me. "No thanks, water is fine."

"No, really. What do you like to drink?" he persists.

I raise the clear plastic in salute and nod with a smile before putting the opening to my lips. Before the other night, I wasn't big on drinking with strangers. Now, I need to be even more vigilant about who I drink with. Cole seems nice and all, he's a great dancer, and he isn't bad looking, but I'm not about to lose my inhibitions with him.

I grab his hand and pull him back to the center of the dance floor. He gives no resistance, and I can make out the faintest sound of his laughter coming over the music. His hands drag down my bare hips. They're cold and send chills down my spine.

"You're a little devil, you know that?" Cole growls into my ear. The little hairs on the back of my neck stand on end.

THE SECRETS THAT WE KEEP

My back presses against his chest as we dance. His hips press into the small of my back as my ass gyrates against the tops of his thighs. He's quite a bit taller than me. Not as tall as the twins or Tate, but he's close.

For a split second, I wonder what those assholes are doing. It must have made Tate's night when he realized I wasn't coming back. The thought rips at my soul, but I push the hurt feelings aside and focus on my dance partner.

I raise my arms over my head, running my fingers through my long hair as I go. My head rolls back against his strong chest. The rhythm of the music hypnotizes me and my lungs fill with the scent of redwoods and leather.

I brace my hands against my partner's warm chest as I grind my ass in sync with the music. His warm, big hands caress my sides and leave a searing trail up the side of my ribs, past my breasts and over my shoulders. Strong hands grip my wrists and turn me around. I press my face into his chest and feel his heart racing against my cheek.

"You've been a bad girl, princess," a familiar voice whispers in my ear from behind me, and I'm hit with the dizzying scent of clove and citrus.

Oh fuck. My eyes fly open and I'm staring straight at the wall that is Tate's chest. What the hell is he doing down here? Where's his fiancee? I turn to move further into the crowd and away from Tate, but Devon blocks my way.

The expression on Devon's face is murderous, and I don't even want to know what Tate looks like. I scan the dance floor for Liam and Aubree. Tate's been an absolute dick to me all evening, but I can't imagine he'd leave his precious little love just to come torment me.

Come to think of it, I can't even see Cole in the throng of sweaty dancers. "What did you do?" I breathe out in a panic.

"What do you mean?" Devon asks with a sinister grin on his face.

"You snuck away to dance, so let's dance." Tate's voice rings in my ear as his strong, hot grip pulls me into his body.

"Where's Cole?" I ask, trying to sound more caring than I actually am. The truth is, I don't really care where he went, what I care about is that these two dickheads are deliberately trying to ruin my night.

"I don't know who Cole is, but the piece of shit who was dry humping your ass won't be coming back any time soon."

THE SECRETS THAT WE KEEP

The possessive growl in Tate's voice snaps something inside my brain and I lose control of myself. Before I can register what I'm doing, I turn to Devon, fisting his gray t-shirt, and I push up on my toes and smash my lips against his. Tate wraps my hair around his big hand and pulls me back.

I turn around, my hair slipping from his grip with ease, and slap him across the face. "Go play with your little Barbie doll, Tate. Leave me alone."

I turn to Devon, glaring at him angrily. "You too, shithead. I've fucking had enough of your games."

This time, when the angry tears threaten to fall, I let them as I storm off the dance floor and make my way to the maze of stairs and levels.

CHAPTER 13

RHYANN

I push past the thin chain curtain and take the first step up when my back is shoved against the wall of the dark stairwell.

"If you run, I'll chase you. Never forget that, Rhyann," Tate says as he breathes down my neck.

"Leave me alone, Tate." I cry, turning my head to look anywhere but at him. "Go find your fiancee and you and Devon can play games with her."

I push at his hard chest, but he doesn't budge. I really should have stayed home and had a slumber party with my sex toys instead of coming out tonight. I never should have trusted Liam or Devon. Every time I trust either one of these men, I'm the one who pays, and it's usually my heart that breaks.

"It's time to go home, Rhyann," Tate commands.

THE SECRETS THAT WE KEEP   163

"Then go." I move my hand to the side, showing him the way up the stairs. "I made a friend, and I need to go find him."

I push past Tate and leave the darkness of the stairs. I know the ladies' room is somewhere nearby. If I can get in there and wait him out, maybe I can find Cole and he can buy me that drink.

The restrooms are in the same place as they are on the other floors, no big surprise there. This one lacks the posh fixtures and romantic feel of the one on the top floor, but it fits the theme of the space well. Corrugated steel lines the walls in the same manner as the bar. In here though, there's graffiti art painted across the walls. Silhouettes of feminine faces with heavy eyeliner and red lips glow under the LED lighting. A red leather couch rests against the far wall of the room.

I consider sitting down and resting there for a moment, but the sticky scent of spilled beer permeates from the slick fabric, turning my empty stomach. Shit. I was so entranced by the adventure this club offered, I forgot to eat something earlier.

With a sigh, I ignore the sticky couch and my empty stomach and pull my phone from my clutch. It's already past midnight. The club should be closing soon, I think.

Bars close at two o'clock, so I imagine nightclubs and speakeasies are held to the same time standard.

I also notice the multitude of missed calls and text messages from the guys. I clear my call history and do a mass delete on all my texts. I don't care to hear or read anything they have to say at this point.

Thinking back on my introduction to Aubree, and the things she said about Adrian and my grandfather's company, *my company*, puts me on edge. I should speak to my grandfather's lawyer in the morning. I barely remember what was in the will anyway. I was too distracted by my grief to really pay attention. I just know that Devereux Publications is mine, and I can take over at the age of twenty-five.

After a few minutes of clearing my head, I peek out the metal door of the ladies' room. The music continues to blast hypnotic beats from the dance floor, but from here, the sounds are muffled and not as alluring. I slip my phone back into my clutch and exit the restroom while digging for my keys in the small purse.

The thing is shallow and has a single pocket. It can't be that difficult to find a set of fucking car keys. My heart jumps into my throat as realization smacks me in the forehead. I don't have my keys. The keys to Donna.

"Devon pulled your keys from your purse when you thought I was your new boyfriend." I jump at the sound of Tate's voice.

He's standing next to me. Right in front of the men's room door. Fucking prick. I should have known I can't ditch him that easily. "My god, what the hell is wrong with you?" I ask him.

I didn't wait for him to answer me; it was a rhetorical question and he's smart enough to know that. Instead, I turn my back to him and make my way for the stairs, for the exit that's three flights up.

It's funny how, when we first arrived, I was so enthralled by this place. I thought the layout and design was innovative, unique. Now, I find it to be tedious and a nuisance. I have to go up three flights, to three different floors, just to get to the stairs that will take me up to another floor so I can take the elevator down. What the fuck was the point in that?

"Rhyann wait," Tate calls from behind me, but I don't listen.

I pull out my phone and dial Devon's number. It goes straight to voicemail. Fuck. I take the steps two at a time, calling Liam next. His also goes straight to voicemail. Mother fuckers. Where is my car? I decide to try Devon again, so I leave a message when the recording picks up. I threaten to do all kinds of horrible, nightmarish things to him if Donna isn't in the space I left her in when we arrived.

I put my phone back into my purse right as I reached the landing at the top of the stairs. The room is a little bit brighter than the stairwell and the floor below. I have to squint my eyes against the light on first entering the room, so I don't see when someone comes up beside me and yanks my arm, dragging me down the hall.

At first I scream and scratch at the hand on my wrist. Then I see that it's Tate, and he's somehow beat me here. Now, he's dragging me off somewhere, and the panic I've been denying over the past couple days starts to set in.

"I hate you," I seethe as Tate shoves me against the wall.

"No you don't," he purrs in response.

I struggle to follow behind him. His hand grips my arm tightly as he pulls me down a hallway and away from prying eyes.

"What the hell is your problem?" I ask when he stops, pinning me to a dark wall.

His steel gray eyes look into mine. A shadow of fear washes over me. I've never seen the look he's giving me. Tate, of all people, has always been kinder, gentler, and at times the most distant with me. That's why I could handle him pushing me away, ignoring me tonight. This, this possessiveness, this ownership he thinks he has over me, it scares me.

"I should be asking you that, princess. What the fuck were you doing leaving us to go dance with some fucking strangers?" His chest rises and falls steadily. My back is up against the cold wall, both of Tate's hands firmly planted on either side of me. He steps closer, so all I can feel, all I can smell or see, is him. Then one hand slides to a small panel on the wall I didn't notice before, and he presses.

The wall behind me begins to shift, opening up to a brushed metal box. A small, brightly lit service elevator.

"What did you plan to accomplish with that stunt, Rhyann? To actually get kidnapped this time?" he asks, pushing me into the small space with him. The doors slide closed before I have a chance to escape.

"It's a service elevator, so you can stop your panicking," Tate says dryly before I can ask him what the hell is going on.

"How did you know where the service elevator was?" My face contorts in confusion.

"It's my club, my building. I'd fucking hope I would know where the service elevator was." Tate laughs mockingly.

We sit in silence the rest of the short trip down. I'm still processing the information, his gray eyes staring into me. His spicy clove and citrus scent fills the box, making it difficult for me to think.

The doors ding and open to the parking garage almost as quickly as they closed when we got on. The smell of rubber and gasoline overpowers Tate's scent, clearing my mind.

"Fuck you, Tate. What the hell is your problem?" I shove at his chest. He loosens his arms around my waist, but his grip on my arm won't let up.

Thick fingers dig into me. I pull away from him, just to be yanked back against the wall of his chest.

"My problem, princess, is that you're being reckless and putting your life and future in danger."

I open my mouth to speak, but the glare in his eyes tells me I should probably bite my tongue.

"You were practically kidnapped not even seventy two hours ago. You should have been home, safe. But

THE SECRETS THAT WE KEEP   169

that's not even safe for you apparently. So, when you're brought out with the only people who can keep you safe, you take off." He goes on, pulling me into the darkness of the parking garage. What did he mean by that? "You decide you want to be a spoiled brat and run away because you're not the center of attention. Then we find you practically fucking some random guy on the dance floor."

"We were dancing." I don't mean for my words to come out so defensive, but I feel attacked by Tate. He's basically implying that I'm being irresponsible and I was the one acting like a spoiled brat. It was his fiancee who wouldn't stop with her childish show of entitlement.

"Where are you taking me?" I ask, stumbling to keep from being dragged, my feet tripping over themselves. My heart begins to beat faster, teetering on the cliff of panic and anger.

"Home." Tate stops in front of a beast on two wheels. Deep red pinstripe details stand out against a solid matte black body. An equally menacing red lightning bolt stares at me from the gas tank.

"Like hell I'm getting on that death trap!" I exclaim, pulling away from him.

Tate lets go of my arm and smiles at me. The wickedness in his eyes glows in the dim lighting of the parking garage.

"It's either you take a ride with me or walk your happy ass all the way back to your house."

He wouldn't. Not after his angry tirade about my safety. "Where's Donna?"

He laughs. "She's safely on her way home right now. Liam's driving her."

I open my mouth to speak and then close it when the words don't come out. No one has driven Donna except for me, my grandfather, and Adrian. The only reason Adrian drove her was because I was unaware that he had her keys.

"Get on," Tate says with a smirk when he realizes he won.

I want to wipe the smirk off his face when he pushes a black helmet into my arms and slips another one over his head. I've never been on a motorcycle before, and my heart races as I attempt to slip the bulbous thing over my head.

Tate turns to me, his face half concealed by the helmet, his stormy eyes glistening with mischief through the open space where his visor will go. He's menacing and sexy as hell sitting on this bike, dressed all in black.

He adjusts the twisted strap under my chin and tightens it. The helmet is heavy and large. I feel like a bobble head, nodding with every little movement. His leather clad fingers gently graze the nape of my neck and around my face, making final adjustments to the helmet.

"All set," he whispers. I could see the corners of his mouth upturned into a smile just before he slid my tinted visor over the opening at my eyes, stealing the light. It's like wearing sunglasses in a dark room. I can make out movement and shapes around me, however the details are muted and hidden in shadow.

I watch as his big form leaves me to straddle the beast on wheels. Once he has himself settled, he reaches for my hands and pulls me to him, patting the back of the seat. I grip his shoulders and lift my leg over the bike, balancing on my toes.

As I settle into the seat behind him, he slides his hands over my legs. First one and then the other, adjusting my legs so they're out of the way of the parts of the bike.

I let out a little giggle, thinking about the old Johnny Depp movie. The musical, where at the end the girl's skirt is ripped off while riding on the back of a motorcycle.

Tate's hands slowly make their way from my thighs to my hips until he finds my hand resting in my lap. With my hand in his, he pulls me forward and wraps my arm around his torso. Taking the hint, I wrap my other arm around and close my hands together.

Why I'm going along with this insane idea with a man who's made it obvious he hates me, I can't say. I just know that the mix of Tate's scent and the smell of the parking garage are hypnotizing, intoxicating.

A part of me fears this drive he's dragging me along for, but another part of me, the part that craves the pain and degradation I could only find in this moment with this man, anticipates the ride.

I don't know what to do with my head, so I rest it on the back of his shoulder. There is a little bit of a jolt as we lift off the kickstand, then smoothly back out and into the lane headed out of the parking garage.

Then it happens. The darkness erupts in a cacophony of thunder as the machine vibrates under me. My thighs tighten, squeezing Tate's big shape, molding myself to his back.

At first we go slow, weaving through the twists and turns of the concrete maze we are parked in. Once we're up and out into the cool air of the city, he takes off, flying through the streets like a bullet fired from a pistol.

"Oh god," I whisper as I feel myself being pulled back by the wind as we cut through traffic. My hold on Tate tightens. His gloved hand rests on mine, giving me a reassuring squeeze.

I close my eyes as we weave through traffic. I can feel myself falling to the side with each twist and turn. After a few minutes we come to a stop, and I brave a peek at the world in front of me.

We're headed out of town going east. Away from the traffic, away from the people and the coast to the west. My hands shake, so I take a few seconds to adjust myself and tighten my grip around Tate.

I'm more anxious over the ride than the destination. There's nothing but darkness around us. The next city over is miles away, but I know what's out there. I'd spent many summers out there growing up. Driving the winding roads in my car, blasting my music with the windows down. It's too late for the streets to be crowded.

The solitude of the ride, the darkness surrounding us, is my solace from the night. An escape from the chaos created by some faceless, nameless entity. Is it too late to ask to get off the ride?

My question is answered by the revving of the engine as the light turns green and I'm jolted back. Again. Dickhead.

"I heard that." His disembodied voice rings through my helmet.

What the hell? Did I say that out loud? How did he hear me? So much has happened so fast in the past twenty minutes, I'm struggling to process everything he said, and everything happening now.

His laugh catches me off guard again and his hand reaches down, tightening around my wrists.

"There's a mic and earpiece in each helmet. So we can communicate," he explains. "Don't let go, princess."

"Oh." I breathe out, resting my covered head on his shoulder. I don't know why, but knowing he can hear me is soothing enough for me to take a breath and watch the scenery pass by in a blur.

It's exhilarating. The wind kissing my skin, the rumble of the engine vibrating underneath me. The power between our legs, and how he has total control over something so fast. I can see why women were attracted to men on motorcycles.

After a while, I get used to riding behind Tate. My body melts into his. His movements become mine as I sway

THE SECRETS THAT WE KEEP

and tilt with him. My heartbeat calms and my breathing matches his.

For whatever reason, I trust him enough to know he won't let me fall. He'll keep me safe while I'm on his bike. Past that I can't be certain anymore, but for this little bit of stolen time, I feel safer here than I've ever been in my life.

CHAPTER 14

RHYANN

After his confession about the microphones, the rest of the ride was fairly silent. I didn't expect to enjoy it as much as I did. It was serene, a peaceful way to clear the mind and still feel the adrenaline of a fast ride. Maybe I'll get myself a bike and learn to ride. I doubt a ride like this will happen again.

The property is dark when we come up the drive on Tate's bike. He cuts the engine at the gate so it doesn't wake Kathleen and Phil. Usually there are lights on along the drive, but for whatever reason, they've been turned off tonight. No big deal. I'm not expecting anyone to show up in the middle of the night, and Tate knows the driveway as well as I do.

The second he stops the bike, Tate hops off and holds out a hand to help me. Without a word, I take it, sliding off the big black beast on wheels. I'm struggling with my

THE SECRETS THAT WE KEEP   177

helmet when a muffled ringing breaks the silence of the
night. I look through the visor as Tate answers his phone.

How the hell did he get his helmet off so quickly?
Thick, deft fingers slide over mine and Tate un-fastens
the strap under my chin before lifting the fiber glass cage
off my head.

"Where's Donna?" I ask, my heart racing as I walk
toward the garage.

Tate grabs me, pulling me to a stop. "She's fine. She's
in the garage, her keys are in the driver's seat. It was Liam
on the phone letting me know the car was there, and that
he and Devon went home."

Oh. I sigh and relax my shoulders a bit. Pulling my
arm from Tate's grip, I change direction and start for the
house.

"Rhyann," Tate calls behind me.

I tune him out. The enchantment of the nightclub and
the thrill of the bike ride has worn off. My mind is as
clear as can be, and I have nothing to say to Tate from
this point on. Tate, Devon, and Liam can all go fuck
themselves, or each other for all I care. I groan, reaching
the front door, as the image of the three of them naked
and sweaty and tangled up in my satin sheets imbeds itself
in my brain.

I go through the front door, something I don't do often, making sure to lock it behind me. I can hear Tate call my name one more time as I close the door. I don't know what to do. I feel like it's been a lifetime since I've said more than a few words to him. I sigh and lean back against the door. The tiny little cracks that have been in my heart for years widen. Cracks formed by Tate and the twins.

But, the days of us being friends, the days of the four of us playing tag on the lawn, are gone. They were gone a long time ago, long before tonight, before Aubree and secret nightclubs. Those days were gone the minute I was sent to Evangeline's School for Girls. That first summer was the first summer that they left me behind. Gemma found a boyfriend, the guys hit puberty hard, and all three had growth spurts. They were in high school, they played sports, and they left me behind.

I rest my head in my hands as I hear the roar of a motorcycle in the distance. Tate isn't as dense as I thought if he got the hint and left. Good. A sob escapes my lips. A small part of me—the part that has been in love with him since my first memories of him—wishes he hadn't left. That was before all the bad things that could happen to a group of kids happened. Before deaths and suicides, before divorces, boarding schools, and murders.

I understand now. I get why Tate didn't want me at his club, with him and the twins. I see why he didn't want me to be a part of that special moment between lifelong friends. I'm not one of them. I haven't been one of them for years, and I never will be again.

The smell of bacon pulls me from my sleep. By the time I made my way from the foyer to my bedroom last night, it was almost sunrise. I slide my feet into a pair of faux fur-lined slippers and make my way down to the kitchen.

Kathleen's just finishing washing dishes when I walk through the swinging doors.

"Mmm, smells good." I sit down at the counter and look over the spread of breakfast foods.

"I'm glad you're up." She looks over her shoulder with a smile. "Someone left roses at the front door for you."

"Really?" My brows arch as I shove a piece of powdered sugar coated French toast into my mouth.

She nods with a soft smile. After my mom died, Kathleen became a motherly figure for me. She was always kind and nurturing. Her and Phil never had children of their own, and I think being able to fill a spot in my life when I needed it most was good for them. For me too. "There's a card, but I didn't want to pry."

I nod and hurry to finish my breakfast, the anticipation killing me. Who would send me roses here? I haven't had a chance to tell anyone about moving back into my grandfather's house.

What if it was Tate, or one of the twins sending roses to apologize for being absolute dickheads last night? The idea of one of those three letting go of their pride has me choking on powdered sugar. I laugh to myself. I don't think a genuine apology exists in their collective vocabulary.

"Kathleen," I speak up after gulping down a big swig of orange juice.

"Yeah, sweetie?" She turns to me, setting the last pan on the drying rack.

I need to figure out my life without Adrian holding my hand, without Tate or Devon or Liam being involved. College was easy. Everything was paid for through the trust my parents had set up, down to the allowance that was deposited into my checking account monthly. Now, everything is different. I need to learn to navigate the

THE SECRETS THAT WE KEEP   181

real world, real business and real life, on my own. I've let everyone, including my late grandfather, shelter me for too long.

"Did Papa keep copies of my parents' wills? Is there a copy of his in the house?" I ask, refusing to let my hopes get too high.

"Of course." Kathleen smiles at me. "Your grandfather kept copies of everything. Birth certificates, death certificates, even your parents' wedding license is in his office. Why do you ask?"

"I don't know," I sigh. "I feel like it's time for me to stop relying on others to manage my life."

"And you think going through all the family papers is a good start?" Kathleen walks over and takes my hands in hers. "I think it's a fantastic idea, honey."

"Thank you," I say with a sad smile.

"You know what, Phil kept your grandfather's laptop." Okay, that's a little weird. I raise my eyebrow, questioning her strange confession. "Don't ask me why. Ask him." She laughs and pulls her phone from her pocket.

An hour later, I'm sitting in my grandfather's old study. Phil brought the laptop. He told me it wasn't password protected. It had been my grandfather's personal computer, and Phil just didn't think it was right that lawyers and auditors were going through our whole lives, putting a price on everything after Papa died.

It brought tears to my eyes, knowing how much Phil and Kathleen have done for me over the years. Papa had to run Devereux Publications, and after my mother died, my father was useless. After his suicide, Papa just didn't know how to raise a little girl on his own. Phil and Kathleen stepped in to help with the things that my grandfather was lost on. Things like bras and periods. Kathleen and Gemma taught me all I needed for that stuff. Phil taught me how to drive, how to throw a punch and shoot a gun. My grandfather was there to give me the love and security I needed. He did everything to ensure I wouldn't need anything for the rest of my life.

"You okay, kid?" Phil asks, pulling me from my thoughts.

I look down at the closed laptop. A small smile curves my lips thinking of all the nights I'd see Papa on the sofa, in this room, typing away on this thing.

"I'm good," I sigh. "I don't know why I've waited so long to do all this."

"Healing takes time," Phil pats me on the head. "Losing someone you love is like losing a piece of your soul, and it takes time for those wounds to heal, kiddo. Kat and I are here if you need us."

Without another word, Phil leaves me to my own thoughts. I set the laptop aside. That's something I can look through in my bedroom, later. What I want now are the papers. Everything that hasn't been digitized. I rummage through the drawers in my grandfather's desk with no luck. All I find there are cheap pens, some paper clips, and the random unused staple or partially dried out rubber band. I'm hoping to find the key to the filing cabinet somewhere in the desk, but after going through every drawer, every corner—I even knocked on the bottoms of drawers hoping for hidden compartments—I come up empty handed.

I'll have to call my grandfather's lawyer in the morning and ask for the documents he has on file. I'm sure he has all of them. I decide to fire up the laptop and see what's on there.

As the tech warms up, I can't help the guilt that creeps into my gut. It's like I'm crossing some invisible line, invading my grandfather's privacy. It's been four years since I saw him, heard his voice, felt his strong arms wrap around me and hug me. My fingers graze the smooth gray plastic keys. It's been just as long since he tapped on these small squares.

The laptop warms up in seconds. The wallpaper on the home screen is the last picture taken of both of my parents and me. I had to have been about eight years old. We were on a mini vacation in Carmel. The wallpaper picture is one Papa took himself, at Carmel Beach. Mom and dad were crouched down on either side of me as we huddled together in a small cave on the beach. Vines of ice plants hung over the mouth of the cave. I smile sadly. I can still remember the faint dripping sounds of water running down its walls.

I'm glad that Phil held onto the laptop. There are so many pictures of my parents and me throughout the years before they died. He had many of the older pictures from before I was born scanned and uploaded onto albums. His wedding to my grandmother—whom I never met. My father's high school and college graduations are here. There are also pictures from my parents' wedding.

Seeing these pictures, reliving some of my favorite early memories, heals a few of those cracks that had been forming in my heart over the years. But a walk down memory lane isn't what I'm after. I'm tired of being in the dark, having everyone do everything for me.

THE SECRETS THAT WE KEEP   185

I find a folder labeled D.P. in the main documents folder. D.P. as in Devereux Publications. Bingo! If I'm to run a major publishing firm in a few months, I better learn whatever I can from the man who built that firm.

Everything in the file is outdated. Most of it is close to ten years old, from before Adrian took over for Papa. Adrian likely has anything up to date—not like I know what I'm looking for. I'm flying blind in all this. I just know I need to get ahead of the game.

I open the web browser next. How long does a person's search history stay on a computer? Especially one that hasn't been used in four years. The cursor hovers over the little compass icon for a second. Do I really want to know what my grandfather googled when I was away at school? Umm, probably not.

I roll the cursor over to the email tab and click that before my curiosity gets the better of me. I start with his inbox, weeding through four years of random spam email. There really isn't anything useful here either. I decide to look at the junk mail. Nothing.

I'm so focused on all the email ads, I don't notice Kathleen coming in with a ham sandwich and a glass of iced tea. She even remembered the barbecue potato chips I've always loved smashed on the inside of my sandwich.

"Find what you're looking for?" she asks, breaking my focus.

"I don't even know what I'm looking for, to be honest," I sigh. "Thank you. You don't have to do all this, you know that right?"

"I know." Kathleen kisses the top of my head. "What do you *think* you're looking for, honey? Maybe I can help. Or Phil might be able to."

"I don't know, really. I'm just tired of Adrian and Tate doing everything for me, running my life. My company. I want to be ready when I can finally take it over."

"Well, why don't you take control now?" She gives me a quizzical look.

"I'm not twenty-five," I state matter of factly.

"So?" She smiles at me.

"Didn't my grandfather's will say I have to be twenty-five?" I ask, confused. I was there the day the will was read, but the day went by in such a haze. I'd lost everyone in my family. I'd never felt so alone in my life until that day. The days between my grandfather's death and the reading of his last will and testament didn't feel so final until I sat down in the lawyer's office. Kathleen and Phil were there, Adrian was there. Those were the only people who shared in my loss. I can't even remember where Tate was, if I think about it. I just know he wasn't with us.

"Darling girl. Adrian merely suggested you wait, and you agreed."

My mouth hangs open slightly in disbelief. I'm a little stunned by what she just said to me, and have to think hard to recall the day. "I don't—I don't remember any of that." Hot tears sting my eyes.

"You wanted legal documents, right, darling?"

I gulp down the knot in my throat and nod my head in response.

"Well, let's go get them." She picks up my plate in one hand—I haven't even touched my food yet—and takes my hand with the other.

"Where are we going?" I ask.

Her smile is warm and comforting. "To the storage room," she laughs. "Do you really think he kept the important documents where people would expect them to be?"

"Well, yeah," I say. "Why wouldn't he?"

"Honey, your grandfather was a genius with money, but he was paranoid," Kathleen explains. "He was always worried about something."

"Really?" I cock an eyebrow. I never noticed my grandfather being paranoid when I was kid.

"Oh yeah," she smirks. "After you went off to boarding school, he packed everything up and locked it away in the storage room."

I don't even know what to say. I stand at the office door, stunned silent. Kathleen gives my arm a little tug and I follow her through the house and into the garage. Donna is sitting there and I look over at her and smile. I love my car, probably more than is healthy, but she's all I have left of my grandfather.

I forgot about the storage room that's off the garage. It was meant to be an above ground wine cellar, windowless and temperature controlled. I never thought my grandfather would use it for anything else.

Kathleen opens the door and pulls the small chain hanging in the middle of the room, a small light bulb flickering on. On either side of the room are vintage bottles of wine. I'm not sure how old they are, or if they're even any good, but I smile because I know, just like Donna, they're a little piece of a past I was too young to appreciate when it was my present. On the floor, against the far wall, are two small plastic filing boxes.

THE SECRETS THAT WE KEEP 189

"I'm sorry I didn't think to tell you sooner. But they're all in here." Kathleen holds my hand, palm up, and places the cellar key in it. "You're the mistress of the house, honey. Your parents and grandfather would be proud of you." She hugs me tightly before she leaves me with the old wine bottles and the answers to questions I don't even have yet.

CHAPTER 15

RHYANN

I lug the boxes to my room and start looking through them. Kathleen was right. I was eligible to take over Devereux Publications as soon as I graduated college. Which is right now. I make a mental note to call my grandfather's lawyer in the morning and let him know I'm stepping into my role immediately. I'll also have to have a meeting with Adrian so it isn't a surprise to him.

I open my grandfather's laptop to send an email to his lawyer. I never finished looking through his files. Should I even bother? I mean, I have everything I wanted in these file boxes. I let my curiosity win this time and click on the sent folder. I scan through the recipient names, not recognizing most of them, but scattered throughout are the last messages he sent to me.

I don't know if I'm ready to open the wound yet, so rather than reliving our old conversations, I click on one that says A.C. I scan through it real quick and realize it's to Adrian. They emailed a lot back then. It seems like most of the emails he sent were to Adrian. In the email, Papa was talking about having dinner with Adrian that night. How he couldn't wait to see him. What? Sure, Adrian was the acting CEO of Papa's company, and my father's best friend, but... I read a little further down—through the conversations and the other emails that the first one I read was a reply to.

They were all so—romantic? Were Papa and Adrian a thing? I never knew my grandmother, and Papa never remarried. Adrian's wife left him years ago, and he never remarried. I gasp, my fingers going up to my lips, suddenly feeling like I've stumbled onto something intimate and private. I hit delete on the email. Obviously, if they were emailing like this, it wasn't something they shared with everyone and it isn't my place to out either of them. Whatever was between my grandfather and Adrian, I just hope they were both happy.

I do the same with the rest of the emails between the two of them. The only emails left in that folder are the ones sent to me and one other email account. I don't recognize this one. There's no telltale signs of who it could be to. So, I click it. The email is dated the day before my grandfather's death, and it's only one sentence long:

"You touch her and they'll never find your body, just like your mother."

I think I'm going to be sick. As I scroll down, I see that there is an entire conversation between my grandfather and the person he threatened. Mostly the other person was sending him some very eerie pictures of me at school, or out with roommates. A couple of them go as far back as my time at Evangeline's.

Above the pictures in what seems to be the first email is the caption: *"Does she know who her REAL parents are?"* What the hell does that mean? Of course I do. My eyes wander over to the second filing box at the foot of my bed. The one I know contains all of our vital records.

Quickly, I click on the other tabs in my grandfather's email. The junk and trash folders have more emails from this mysterious sender. Most threaten to expose my grandfather in one way or the other, but the ones that catch my eye are the two that talk about legitimacy. Bile rises in my stomach as I click on each one and read through. The sender claims to be the biological child of Lenora and Garrett Devereux. That my grandfather knew him and knew he was his true heir, true grandchild.

Impossible. Lenora was a Crawford, she married Adrian. And my mother's name was Sophia.

With shaking hands I close the laptop and reach for the second file box. The one that'll prove this psychopath wrong. The first paper I pull out is my father's death certificate. I already know the gory details so I don't need to read it. Next is my mother's death certificate. Then, their marriage certificate. I pull out every single sheet of embossed paper. My grandmother's death certificate. There's even Adrian and Lenora's divorce filings in here. But not my birth certificate. What the hell?

In a fit of panic, I pull my phone out and call my grandfather's lawyer.

"Hello?" the voice on the other end says hesitantly.

"Mister Montgomery, this is Rhyann Devereux," I speak clearly.

"Oh, hello Rhyann. Please call me Calvin." His voice sounds cheerful, friendly. "What can I do for you?"

I hesitate for a second, shaking off the haze of panic. "I was wondering if you had a copy of my birth certificate. Also I'd like to take my place at my company effective immediately."

"I don't have a copy of the birth certificate, but I do have your adoption records on file."

The room spins and I do everything I can to hold back from throwing up all over the place. My uneaten sandwich from earlier taunts me as I try to focus on the mess around my bed. "Adoption?" I ask.

"Yes, your ado—" he stops, sighs, and clears his throat. "I take it no one told you. James didn't say anything before he died."

There's a tinge of regret in his tone. My heart sinks as hot tears roll down my cheeks. "No one told me anything about adoptions." I try to hide the pain from my voice. "Was I adopted?"

"Look, I'm at the office getting some weekend work done, I'm just about to wrap up. Why don't we meet for coffee in twenty minutes? I'll bring everything I have for the Devereux estate, including the paperwork for you to begin taking control of Devereux Publications."

I nod my head, speechless. But he can't see me so I take a deep breath and force my vocal cords to work for a minute. I choke out, "Okay," and then hang up the phone.

Twenty minutes later, I'm sitting at a table in the corner of the coffee shop down the street from Calvin's office. I decided to bring my grandfather's laptop to ask if Calvin knows anything about what was written in those emails. I have to trust that my grandfather's long time friend and lawyer would be open and honest with me. The estate has been paying him to be on retainer as my personal lawyer since my grandfather died. Not that I've been in need of legal services, or plan to any time soon.

Calvin arrives ten minutes after me. He's about average height, thin, with a head full of silvery hair. He's clean shaven and doesn't look dressed like he just came from the office. He's wearing a pair of black shorts that fall to his knees and a loose fitting black tank top. A splatter of silvery chest hairs wink up at me from the neckline of his top. He's not bad looking for an older man.

"Rhyann, it's good to see you." He smiles and sets his messenger bag down on the wooden tabletop. "I think the last time I saw you was the reading of your grandfather's will."

He's correct. I haven't seen him since that day. "I think it would be a little concerning if you had," I laugh, my attempt at making a joke. A bad joke. "I haven't been in need of a lawyer."

"Well, that's a good thing. Isn't it?" He laughs back and sits down across from me. "I'm so sorry you had to find out about the adoption like this."

"It's okay." I give him a weak smile. I'm still reeling from his revelation.

"No, it's not. Your grandfather wanted to tell you before he died." Calvin sighs. "He would be furious if he knew I told you by accident."

I never knew much about Calvin Montgomery. Growing up, Papa didn't have a whole lot of parties at the house. I just knew Calvin was my grandfather's friend and lawyer. So, it's difficult for me to discern whether or not he's being genuine. His words sound genuine, and the soft, sad look in his eyes emphasizes the tone in his voice.

"So, why didn't anyone tell me? Adrian's had opportunities since Papa died."

Calvin clears his throat and opens the leather bag sitting in front of him. "To my knowledge, Adrian doesn't know." He pulls a thick manila folder out and slides it over to me. "Nobody but your grandfather, parents, and myself knows. The adoption was private and your birth parents' identities were never disclosed."

I take the offered envelope and set it on the table with a quiet nod. "Well, somebody knows, and they were threatening my grandfather before he died," I say, opening the laptop and turning it so Calvin can read the suspicious emails.

Calvin's hazel eyes shift from left to right as he reads the email on the screen. I know he's finished one when his hand runs across the touchpad in a scrolling motion. After a few minutes of him repeating the same motions, Calvin looks up at me, sadness and concern in his eyes.

"Rhyann I'm sorry," he sighs. "Your grandfather never told me about this."

I was afraid of that. Deep down, I had a feeling this was another secret my grandfather kept from me, from everyone. "Well, what am I supposed to do?" I ask.

Calvin gives me a tight smile, "There's nothing we can do with those emails. However, if you get any strange or threatening messages, call me and the police immediately."

"Do you know about the attempted kidnapping?" I ask, assuming he was unaware, considering his instructions.

His eyes grow wide and he shakes his head. "I did not. Are the police involved?"

I recount the events of the other night and the interview with the detectives the following day. I explained that the car I was found in was registered in my father's name, and the police asked when I saw him last. The sarcastic laugh that escaped my lips when I described the conversation was automatic.

"I think you need to show the police these emails, Rhyann," Calvin says when I finish with my story. "As your lawyer, I'm advising you to turn the laptop over to detectives."

I'm crestfallen at the idea of giving the police my grandfather's laptop. It's one of the only connections I have left of him, one of the last things he touched. Calvin must be able to sense my rising panic. His arm reaches across the table and cups my trembling fingers in his warm hands.

"Rhyann, I'll make sure you get it back, if that's what you want," he reassures me.

"Thank you," I sigh. I deleted the conversations between my grandfather and Adrian, so I'm not too concerned with invading the men's privacy. "Can I just keep it for one more night? I'll give it to you tomorrow."

Calvin gives me a small smile and nods in the affirmative.

"Well, hello beautiful."

Calvin's eyes shift from the laptop in front of him to just above my head. I figured the voice behind me was someone meeting their girlfriend or something. Awkwardly, I shift in my seat to see who my older companion is looking so intently at.

"Never thought I'd get the chance to buy you that drink," the tall, dark haired man smiles down at me. There's something vaguely familiar about his pitch black gaze. It takes a minute for it to register in my brain. Last night! My mysterious dance partner who suddenly disappeared on me.

"Cole, right?" I ask, breaking the awkward staring contest between the two of us.

"You remembered my name." He smiles down at me. He does have a nice smile. It softens the harsh lines of his jaw and the jagged knit on the bridge of his nose.

"Well, Miss Devereux." Calvin clears his throat. I look back at my companion as he closes the laptop and slides it in front of me. "I'll keep you updated on the progress of our situation."

"Thank you, Mister Montgomery," I nod with a smile.

Calvin stands and pushes in his chair, his back rigid and straight. I don't know the man well, but he's always seemed so relaxed and at ease. Right now, though, he seems anything but that.

Before he can leave, I stand up. "Wait, Calvin." I reach for his arm and he looks at me with a soft gaze. "What about—"

"It's fine," he cuts me off. I don't miss the quick glance at the man behind me. "I'll speak with Mister Crawford, and we will get started on the transition."

I nod when Calvin pats the back of my hand.

His voice is hushed as he says, "For now, let's keep everything, I mean everything, we discussed between the two of us."

I nod again in understanding.

"Have a good day, Miss Devereux." Calvin smiles one last time and walks out the glass doors of the small shop.

"Let me buy you a coffee," the deep voice behind me says. "Since I didn't get to buy you that drink last night."

I almost forgot Cole was behind me. "I'm sorry, Cole. Not today." I try to be polite as I gather my things to leave.

A strong hand grips my arm tightly. "Come on," he coaxes. "You left without a word last night." Last night, he disappeared from the crowd when Tate showed up on the dance floor. I just assumed he moved on to someone more interested in his flirtations.

I look into his dark eyes. There's something mesmerizing about them, like I'm looking into a deep, empty well and if I stare too long, I'll fall and never stop falling into darkness.

I sigh. "I'm sorry about last night, but I really do have to go right now." I slip my phone into my purse and sling it over my shoulder. I move to pull my arm from Cole's grip. His fingers dig into the muscle as he tightens his grip.

"Then let me take you to dinner tonight," he offers when I pull my arm free.

"Cole, I can't." My eyes fall to my shoes while I gather the file and the laptop. "I'm sorry."

"Sure you can." His tone is deeper now. Searing heat radiates off his body as he consumes the space between us. A sick feeling bubbles in my stomach. I turn to walk past him when his arm wraps around my waist. "Don't leave me again, Rhyann."

His words are barely above a whisper, but there's something eerily haunting in his tone that sends shivers down my spine. "Cole, I—"

"She said she's unavailable tonight," an angry voice growls. I look up and into the crystalline blue of Devon's eyes. If Cole's eyes are a bottomless pit of darkness, Devon's eyes are an eternally bright, unpredictable blue sky.

"Mind your own business." Cole looks back at Devon with a poisonous stare. "The lady can do what she likes."

"I never said she couldn't." Devon smirks. "I just repeated her words, since you don't care to listen when they're coming out of her mouth."

I want to laugh. Since when did Devon ever take his own advice? "If the two of you will excuse me, I need to get home." I push past Cole and Devon as the two of them stare each other down like two dogs fighting over the same piece of meat.

Long, thin fingers wrap around my arm—again—and stop me from making my way to the exit.

"Rhyann," Cole breathes against my cheek. He's so close, I can make out the rancid smell of stale cigarettes mixed with peppermint.

I yank my arm from his grip one last time before daring to stare up into the blackness of his gaze. "Don't touch me again," I tell him in as firm a voice as I can muster. Without another word, I push past Cole, my eyes locked on the exit, and out the door.

I don't look back to see if Devon followed behind me, and frankly I don't really care. I'm unsure of what he was doing at the coffee shop to begin with, but I have no interest in waiting to find out. I just want to go home.

Chapter 16

Rhyann

When I come up the gravel drive, Tate's car and Liam's jeep are parked in front of the house. I groan as I step out of Donna and make my way to the front door. If I'm going to be living here, and allowing the Morris brothers to manage my security, then I'm going to have to set some ground rules with them—and Tate.

I make it through the foyer, down the hall past the formal living room, and past the kitchen and dining room. I'm about to ascend the stairs to the safety of my bedroom when a deep male voice calls to me from the game room.

"Well, hello princess," Liam says, holding a maple and onyx pool cue at his side like it's some type of magical staff and he's guarding a sacred cavern.

"Not now Liam," I sigh, the weight of my meeting with Calvin finally settling on my shoulders.

"Did you just roll your eyes at me?" he growls.

How the hell did he see that? I'm not even looking at him. My eyes lock on the edge of the rug at the top of the stairs. It's only a few feet away. The last thing I need is to have to face Liam and Tate.

As soon as I think of Tate's name, my ears pick up the deep rumble of his laughter from the game room. I can't help but wonder what he's laughing at, then I hear light feminine giggles. Aubree. Tate's—I shudder a cringe—fiancee. The girl who thinks her fiance is going to run my company someday. I laugh and turn to face Liam, a sinister smile stretching across my face.

"Is Tate in there?" I ask sweetly.

Liam looks me over. He knows my facial expressions, he knows my thoughts better than anyone. "Are you thinking about causing trouble, princess?"

"Aren't I always?" I wink and make my way to the game room. As I pass by, I reach out and take Liam's hand in mine, our fingers interlacing. Stopping for just a moment, I push up on my toes and plant a kiss on his clean shaven cheek. My lips linger, breathing in the scents of citrus and sage on his skin.

"Umm, Rhy," Liam whispers, holding his position in the doorway.

"Nothing's changed between us, Liam," I clarify.

I need to keep the boundaries I set with him. What happened between us when my grandfather died, that year we spent fighting and fucking, the feelings I had for him, need to stay buried along with everything else I lost back then, everything I loved.

"Rhyann," Liam whispers, the sadness in his voice mirroring my own.

"You said yourself, it was just casual, remember?" I ask, pulling my arm from his grip and making my way into the game room. We have baggage, secrets shared between us that neither Tate nor Devon know about.

"Stop it, it's my turn." Aubree's shrill, whiny voice bounces off the walls of the game room. She's at the pool table, a woman's cue in her hand. Tate sits behind her in one of the high leather stools that are spread out along the room. Every time Aubree pulls back on her cue to take aim at the white ball on the table, Tate taps the end with the toe of his boot.

I hide my snicker as I observe the scene, unnoticed by the couple. Tate's getting enjoyment out of her annoyance. I am too, to be honest. He smiles wickedly every time she has to stop because of him, a glimmer of amusement in his eyes.

THE SECRETS THAT WE KEEP

"You know what." Aubree slams the cue down on the table. "I'm done. I don't want to play if you want to be a creep like that."

As she folds her arms over her chest and pouts, Tate's gaze shifts from his childish fiancee to me. His eyes darken, and the smile slowly fades. What the fuck did he expect? This is my house. If he wants to be here, he's going to have to see me.

"Fine, Rhyann can take your turn," Tate says in a low, menacing voice.

I glare at Tate, trying to figure out what game he's playing with Aubree and me. Whatever it is, I'm not so sure I like it.

"No, fuck that," Liam says, sauntering up next to me. "She's on my team, we're evenly stacked now."

I look over at Liam and laugh. "I am not on your team. You're worse than he is." I nod my head in Tate's direction. The guys aren't bad at the game, and they know it. We all grew up learning the game on this table. When we were kids, they had moments when they were better than me. It usually had to do with our sizes at that time. But as I got older, and the more time I spent alone here during my holidays home, the more skill I gained.

My college friends thought it was a neat party trick for the petite little redhead to school all the drunken frat boys at the pool table.

"And what makes you think you're better than I am?" Tate stands up, reaches around Aubree, and takes the smaller pool cue from the table and extends it to me.

Aubree just stares at him, red faced and wide eyed. Then her head snaps in my direction, shiny blonde curls slapping her in her perfect, porcelain cheek. "What are you doing here?" she asks with a sneer.

I clutch my sides as laughter starts to roll out of me. I can't help it, I just laugh as Aubree's already red face grows even redder.

"What's so funny?"

I can't find the breath to answer her. I don't even know if I have an answer to her question. What *is* so funny? I suck air into my lungs, holding one finger up asking for a moment. "What are *you* doing here?" I ask, finally catching my breath. My brow quirks as I watch her expression shift from anger to confusion and back to anger. Before she can finish, I add, "Please, tell me. Did Tate tell you this was his house too?"

"Don't be ridiculous." Aubree looks annoyed as her gaze goes from me to Tate and back to me. "I've been to Tate's apartment millions of times. I just don't know what you're doing *here*."

"Why wouldn't I be here?" I ask. "It's my house." I raise my brows at Tate. I have no idea who he told her I am, or what my connection to him and the twins is. When Liam lets out a soft laugh next to me, I know I'm not the only one who finds the shift in her expression amusing.

"So, you're their client and their fuck toy?" Aubree asks with disgust, glaring at Liam beside me.

A slow smile stretches across my face. Tate and Liam both pale in shock. Tate reaches his hand out to grab Aubree's shoulder as I slowly make my way to her.

"Honey, if I were their fuck toy, the twins wouldn't be the only ones climbing into my bed." I push Aubree out of the way with my hip and take the pool cue out of Tate's hand. "Now, if you will kindly get the fuck out of my way, I'll show you how to play pool before I kick you out of my house."

"I know how to play," she whines behind me.

Before I decide which shot to take, I slowly walk around the table, studying the positions of each numbered ball, the cue ball, and the eight ball. All fifteen balls remain on the table. Whoever broke is a shitty shot. I look up to see all three of my unwanted guests staring intently at me. The fuckers were playing nice for Aubree.

"Anyone care to place a wager?" I ask no one in particular.

I hear two deep male voices say 'no' in unison as the only other female voice smugly says 'yes'.

I laugh and walk up to Aubree to look her in the eyes. "What are you willing to lose, Goldilocks?"

She squares her shoulders and flicks her hair back. "Who says I'm going to lose?"

"Rhyann, stop this." Tate all but growls behind his fiancee.

I roll my eyes, ignoring him, and stare down this spoiled brat who thinks she can walk into my world and take what's mine. For a split second, my heart speeds up and threatens to burst out of my chest. Tate isn't really mine, he never was. The forceful beating is replaced with something more like a fissure forming, like when cracks form in dry dirt or cement. If those were living things, I imagine that's what this would feel like.

I shake off the unwanted emotions and clear my throat. "So, what are you willing to bet, Aubree?" I ask, holding my empty hand up, looking around my game room. "Money? Cars? What are you willing to lose if I win?"

"Them," she says with a self righteous smirk.

"Excuse me?" I laugh.

"If you lose the game, then you find a new security team and never see your twin boyfriends again." The way she says *twin boyfriends* makes me want to laugh.

"And if I win?" My eyebrows arch in amusement.

"If you win, which I'm certain you won't." She's an arrogant bitch, her hands gripping her hips, her chin tilted upward, and her eyes staring down at me. "I'll call off the engagement."

"What?" Tate stands up, his jaw nearly hitting the floor in shock. "Aubree, don't be ridiculous."

"I accept." I smile and turn back to the table. Poor Tate. I tune his voice out as he argues with his fiancee over the bet we just made. Looking over the table, I see what I'm sure he's already figured out. I could easily win this in one shot if I tried.

Before I can take my first shot, Devon appears in the doorway, fury written across his hard features. "So, this is what you assholes do while I'm working?"

"It's getting good, bro. Aubree just bet her engagement on the game." Liam laughs. I'm glad I'm not the only one who finds it amusing.

I look up and smile at Devon and he gives me a scowl in return.

"Talk some sense into her, Dev," Tate says as his best friend joins us by the pool table. "Rhyann accepted the bet."

Devon comes to stand beside me, looking over the game. "She'd have been dumb not to," he says with a deep laugh. "Besides, who broke that?"

"Tate did," Liam offers up almost immediately.

"Hmm, well you're fucked," Devon replies.

Done with the back and forth over the wager, I turn and look Tate in the eyes. "Let's make this a little more interesting," I say with a wicked smile.

"Rhyann," Tate says, his tone warning me. Finally he stands and walks toward me. "Don't do this." He's so close, I can feel the heat of his breath against my skin. "Please."

"Why? I'd hate to lose the best security team in town." I look past him to Aubree. "Don't you own shares in your daddy's company, Goldilocks?"

"I like that nickname," Devon snickers, earning him a deadly glare from Tate's fiancee.

"Yeah, so?" she asks.

THE SECRETS THAT WE KEEP   213

"If I win in one turn, you'll give me half your shares,"
I answer.

"Ha! Like that's even possible. You're on."

"Don't you want to know what you'd get if I don't
clear the table?" I quirk a brow in her direction.

"No," she smirks. "I know it's impossible. The balls are
scattered all over the table. I'm so confident you can't do
it, I don't want anything from you. Besides, it's not like
you have anything of equal value to offer anyway."

"Okay." I smile and turn back to the table.

"This is bullshit," Tate growls behind me. "Aubree,
stop this. Call off the fucking bet."

"Why? She won't win," she whines.

I tune them out as they continue to argue behind me
and focus on the balls on the table. "Three ball, right
center pocket," I call out before taking my shot. As I
expected, the ball goes right into the called pocket with
ease. Next I call the seven ball, and as I planned, it goes
right into the pocket I meant for it to go into.

My turn goes like this, me calling the ball and a pocket
and not missing a single shot, until all that's left are the
striped balls and the eight ball. With a confident smirk, I
turn and wink at Aubree.

"Ugh. I get it, you're good." She rolls her eyes. "Now, please, make your final shot."

I laugh. "Who said this was my final shot?"

Devon snorts, Liam laughs out loud and Tate just stares at me, hatred burning in his gray eyes. "Stop with the showboating and get this over with," he growls.

I sigh and lock eyes with him. "You know, no one asked you to come here, and no one is keeping you here." I point to the door with the chalky tip of my pool cue. "You and your fiancee are welcome to leave at any moment."

"I don't need your permission to leave," Tate says dryly.

"No, but you do to stay, and I don't want you here." I turn back to the table without giving him another glance and sink the rest of the balls, including the eight ball at the end.

"Well, Aubree." I turn to the woman who is quietly whining to Tate about the outcome of the bet she made. "I won, my lawyer will contact your father Monday regarding the shares of his company. Now, get the fuck out of my house."

I lean back against the edge of the pool table, my arms folded over my chest as I wait for her to register the words I spoke.

"You cheated!" She screams, and it takes more energy than I'd hoped to keep from visible cringing. "I'm not giving you anything!"

"You know, I'm not even bothered by that." I smile calmly. "You can keep your company, your fiancee, and go. I didn't want visitors today anyway."

I lay the mahogany stick atop the merlot colored felt and walk out of the room, stopping at the door. I turn to Devon. "If you really do work for me, I want my house and property empty before I get out of the bath and come back down for a drink."

Chapter 17

Rhyann

An hour later, I'm not disappointed to find the entire house empty and silent when I leave my bedroom. I admit, it was a bitch move—not the part where I flaunted my impressive billiards skills—when I asked the twins to make sure everyone left, but I'm over being handled by the men in my life. I'm done letting any of them tell me how to live my life, and when and where to do things.

The cabinet door closes with a loud clap as the two pieces of wood hit each other. My body flinches, half expecting my grandfather to come in reminding me not to slam the cabinets shut.

I fill a tray with cold cuts, meats, cheeses, a sliced apple, and some carrots. Tucking a bottle of wine under my arm, I grab a glass and take my bounty into the family room. I'm used to being alone. Having the twins here—and Tate— lately is out of my comfort zone.

THE SECRETS THAT WE KEEP   217

Shadows dance and play across the walls of the family room as the sun sets outside. I love this time of day, when it isn't dark enough for the lights to come on, but the sky begins to freckle with stars.

I leave my food on the coffee table and take my wine to the patio. It's still early June, so the summer heat hasn't set in yet, and it's a beautiful evening. I settle into one of the cushioned wicker chairs and watch the sky shift from blue to gold to magenta as the sun sinks further in the sky. I'm too far from the bay to be able to watch the sun slip into the ocean, but I've seen an ocean sunset enough times to picture its magnificence in my mind.

Behind me, the sound of the floorboards moaning echoes through the house. That's odd. I know I'm alone. Kathleen and Phil are off, the twins are doing whatever it is they do when they aren't making my life miserable, and god knows what Tate and Aubree are up to.

I turn and look through the French doors and confirm what I already knew. I'm alone, just like I've been for the majority of my life. I shake off the self pity and turn back to enjoy the sunset and my glass of wine. I hate the idea of blindsiding Adrian tomorrow, but I can't help the feeling that he's been lying to me, keeping secrets from me, and that he's trying to keep me from my own company.

That self pity is replaced by bitter anger and feelings of betrayal. The only father figure left in my life has delegated my safety to his son's best friends while he traipses around Northern California, running the company my grandfather left in his care until I was ready to take over. Now, he's trying to change the rules and keep me from taking my rightful place in Devereux Publications.

With an angry growl, I stand up and resist the urge to hurl my wine glass over the patio railing into the lawn. The wrought iron rail is cool to the touch when I walk up and grip it in my free hand. The fresh evening air fills my lungs and I'm reminded of the summers I'd come home from boarding school and Papa would have every possible summer activity set up for me on the back lawn. Never mind the fact that we have a gorgeous swimming pool with a concrete water slide. He wanted me to enjoy my summers at home with him, when he wasn't too busy working or doing whatever networking or charity event he had to attend for the company. My company.

With a new resolve, I walk back into the family room. I was going to watch a movie and hopefully fall asleep on the couch, but the sound of the front door banging against the wall draws my attention to the entryway.

"Liam, you better not be messing with me," I call out into my empty house. "Dev, I'm not in the mood tonight."

I swear, if those assholes are messing around, I'm going to kill them. Then I'm going to find a whole new security company to handle things for me, after I hire someone else to get rid of their hulking, albeit sexy, bodies. *Sexy? Ew. What the fuck is wrong with me?* I ask myself. I don't really think the twins are sexy, do I?

I set my wine glass on the coffee table next to the plate of food. My eyes catch the uneven number of apple slices sitting there. Now, I'm not OCD, not to the point of counting out all my pieces of food, but I haven't had a chance to eat any of it, and I know I cut eight slices of apple. I cut it in half and then, logically, I cut each half into quarters. So, why are there only seven slices?

"Alright guys. This is bullshit," I call out into the silence. "Quit fucking around. If you really want to stay, you can."

When I'm answered by a deafening silence, save for the echoing footsteps in some room across the house, the hairs on the back of my neck stand on end. Liam and Devon would never think to mess with my head like this.

Not after Friday night, not with whoever tried to kidnap me still out there.

I pick up my phone and call Liam.

"Hey princess, what's up?" he answers on the second ring.

"Are you guys in the house?" I ask, getting straight to the point.

"What are you talking about Rhyann?" Laughter and a hint of concern linger in his tone.

"Stop fucking with me, Liam. Either you or Dev came in and snuck one of my apple slices, and I can hear you running through the rooms right now. "

"Rhyann, we aren't there, I swear." Devon's tone is a little more harsh, curt. "No one should be in the house but you."

While he continues talking to me, I walk down the hall toward the sound of footsteps. The sounds are coming from my grandfather's study. The very same study I searched this morning for any records about my family, my birth, and my grandfather's will.

The door is ajar, and I can hear whoever they are pulling drawers open, slamming cabinets shut. "Well, if it's not you two, then who is in the office going through my grandfather's shit?" I ask.

"Rhyann, listen carefully," Devon says calmly. "Get out of the house. Now. Run to Phil and Kathleen's cottage. We're on our way."

"Knock it off, you're just trying to scare me." I roll my eyes, pushing the door open a little more. "If it's not you two, it's probably Tate, messing with me to get me back for making his stupid girlfriend look even dumber than she already looks."

The hinges betray me and creak as the door opens slightly. A tall figure in a red hoodie is hunched over my grandfather's desk, pulling out the drawers and emptying the contents onto the desktop. He freezes in place over the desk and looks in the direction of the door. My direction.

Shit! I back away from the door, my heart racing. "Someone's in the office," I whisper into the phone.

"Get the fuck out of the house, Rhyann," Devon growls into the phone. "We're almost there."

The person in the office starts for the door, in the same direction where I stand frozen in shock. Quickly, I back away and head for the front door, Devon and Liam still on the phone. My heart is pounding and my hands shake as I make my way through the house. My house, my one safe place. Hot tears sting my eyes, a startling contrast to the cool evening air hitting my face as I cross the threshold and make it out the front door.

"I'm outside." I try to keep the panic from my voice as I breathe heavily into the speaker. "I think the person saw me, I don't know."

"It's okay, don't panic," Liam says softly. "Run down to Kathleen's. Dev sent Phil a text. He's going to meet you halfway."

I nod—not like he could see me nod—and begin running down the gravel driveway that connects the main house to the cottage Phil and Kathleen live in. It doesn't take long for me to see the dark silhouette along the path. Within seconds I'm crying into Phil's chest as he takes the phone from my hand.

"I've got her, boys," Phil says into the phone. "Uh huh. No, I don't see any unfamiliar vehicles. Yeah, I'm gonna take her to my place until you give the all clear. Yup." Phil ends the call and smoothes out my now matted mess of hair. "Shh, it's okay kiddo. Let's get you inside." He doesn't let go as he guides me to his house and his sweet wife who has always treated me like I was one of her own children.

Chapter 18

Rhyann

Phil gets me settled in his kitchen as Kathleen puts on a pot of coffee.

"She doesn't need coffee, wife. She needs a stiff drink," Phil says to Kathleen with a devious little smile.

"Maybe so." Kathleen looks at me and smiles warmly. "That's why I have this."

Kathleen pulls a bottle of Bailey's Irish Cream Liqueur out of the cabinet above her stove.

"Sneaky sneak," Phil chuckles. "That's why I love you, woman." He kisses his wife on the cheek and sits down on the stool next to me. Phil slides my phone across the marble countertop. I'd completely forgotten about it once I felt safe.

I pick it up and look at the screen. There's a text from Devon letting me know he and Liam just pulled up to the main house. I hope whoever was in the house is gone by now. I didn't wait to find out if they had a weapon on them. I don't even know what they looked like.

My teeth begin to chatter as chill runs down my spine. How could someone break into my house, without me knowing, without it triggering the alarm system? What were they looking for in my grandfather's study?

My heart stops for just a second as the answers hit me on the forehead. *Oh, my god.* "Did you guys know I was adopted?" I ask softly.

Kathleen stops what she's doing over by the stove and turns around to face me. Phil clears his throat but keeps his eyes on the counter. "It was never meant to be a secret, Rhyann."

"Phil," Kathleen warns.

"No, she needs to know." He chooses now to look at me, and there's sadness written all over his aging features. "Your mother couldn't have children, but your father, he wanted a house full of babies."

Kathleen pours three cups of coffee, and before handing one to me, she adds a decent amount of Bailey's into my cup. I take the offered drink with a small nod as Phil continues his story.

"One day, your mother met a young woman at the clinic she'd been going to for her cancer treatments. The

THE SECRETS THAT WE KEEP

girl was barely seventeen years old, alone and out of money. She was also three and a half months pregnant." He pauses and looks at me. Understanding washes over me and I gulp down a mouthful of the spiked coffee. "They came to an agreement. Your parents would give the girl a place to stay, feed her, get her the best doctors and care money could buy during her pregnancy. Then, after the baby was born, they'd adopt the baby, and pay her a hundred thousand dollars to keep the adoption a secret."

"Did she?" I don't know why I asked that. Obviously she didn't. Someone out there knows the truth.

"She never got the chance," Kathleen speaks up. "The poor girl died giving birth."

"Besides your parents, grandfather, and us, the only person who knew about your biological mother was Lenora," Phil finishes.

And there's the connection. Somehow, I know in my gut, Tate's mother and father are connected to all of this. "So, is it possible her and Adrian told someone else?"

Phil bites his lip. "Hmm, I guess it's possible Lenora told Adrian at some point before the divorce."

"Wait." I look from Phil to Kathleen then back to Phil. "Adrian didn't know?"

"Adrian spent that year in Seattle getting the offices there up and running. When young Sybil died, your grandfather felt the less people who knew about it, the better."

"Sybil," I sigh. That was my mother's name. Not Sophia, Sybil. A fissure forms in my chest, and my heart breaks a little for the young mother who never got to see the baby she brought into the world. She never got the chance to experience all the things a young adult experiences, all the heart breaks, the friends, the fights. She died before she had the chance to live.

Tears hang on my lashes, ready to fall to the cool counter when there's a knock on the door.

"I'll get it. It's probably the boys." Phil stands up and walks out of the room.

"Are you okay, honey?" Kathleen asks me, wrapping my shaking hands in hers.

"Yeah," I assure her. "This is all just a lot to take in."

"I know it is, but your grandfather raised you to be a smart, strong woman. You can handle so much more than you think you can." Her smile comforts me. She may not realize it, but there were times in my childhood when she and Phil were more like parents to me than my own parents or grandfather.

"Thank you," I whisper.

I take another sip of coffee as Phil returns, Liam and Devon behind him.

"Someone was definitely there," Liam tells us.

"No shit." I roll my eyes. "I saw the person."

"Did you see their face?" Devon asks.

"No," I answer quietly with my head down, my eyes locked on the swirling brown liquid inside the mug in front of me.

"Like I was saying." Liam ignores my shameful admission. "Whoever they were, they were looking for something. They trashed the office and Rhyann's bedroom."

"My bedroom?" I ask, looking up in shock. "Why my bedroom?"

I take mental note of everything I own, everything in my bedroom that might be of value to anyone other than me. I really don't have anything. I'm not a materialistic person.

"They were probably looking for money or jewelry, honey," Kathleen offers.

"But I don't really have any jewelry." I look at Devon. "Did they touch anything?"

"Not that we noticed. Your purse and backpack were dumped out on the bed, though."

My backpack? *Oh my god.* The laptop. My grandfather's laptop, and the files from Calvin. Whoever it was, they were not there to hurt me, at least not at the moment. They were there for information.

"I have to go." I push away from the counter, hopping off the stool.

"Go where?" Liam asks, a concerned look in his eyes.

"I have to go back to the house. Now."

"Rhyann, I think we need to call the police," Phil interjects. "What if this was the same person who tried to kidnap you?"

"Phil, I'm almost certain it is, and that's why we cannot call the police just yet." Liam and Devon both look at me expectantly, as if they're waiting for an explanation. I know I owe them one. I owe Kathleen and Phil a better explanation also, but I don't have one. I just know in my gut that the only people I can trust are in this kitchen right now. "Please, trust me. If they took what I think they did, then they're gone and I'm not in any more danger tonight."

I'm a little surprised that it's Kathleen who speaks up. She's always been the observer, the mother hen who watches over her chicks. "What is it you think they took, honey?"

I stare deep into her blue eyes, faded with age, but still as bright with energy as they were when I was a kid. "My grandfather's laptop and the files from the lawyer."

I don't need to elaborate for the older couple to grasp the gravity of what may have been stolen. While my adoption was not meant to be kept a secret from me, it wasn't something my parents or grandfather wanted to be public knowledge.

"It's possible." Liam interrupts the silence. "There was no laptop in the room that we were able to see."

"I need to go back to the house to see if this stuff is missing, but why don't you want us to call the police if you're sure the thief and the kidnapper are the same person?" Devon growls, his face contorted into a snarl, his big arms folded tightly across his chest.

I sigh. I have no idea what to say to them or how to explain it. I don't even know if I'm crazy or not, but this feeling has been building up in my gut since this afternoon, and the more that happens, the more I think about everything that's been said and done in the past few days, this feeling gets stronger.

Everything in the living room is as I left it. My glass of wine half full, my platter of finger foods untouched. I shake my head and make my way to my bedroom. I left everything there when I got home today. I put the laptop and files safely under my bed. Well, I assumed they'd be safe there, but I also never expected to have someone break into my house looking for them.

My bedroom door is closed when we make our way up the stairs and down the long hallway. Devon and Liam are right there, next to me. As I reach out to grab the door knob, Dev takes my hand.

"You don't have to do this," he tells me, his voice low and controlled. "I can go in and look for the laptop and files for you."

"I can't let anyone control me, Dev." I offer him a tight smile. "I can't be afraid forever."

"Rhyann," he sighs quietly before letting go of my hand.

I'm so stunned by his tenderness, I stand frozen for a moment. When I turn the knob and open the door, I'm not prepared for the destruction I walk into.

My bed has been torn apart, the comforter and sheets torn from the mattress—which has been ripped to shreds— and what looks like the entirety of my closet is

THE SECRETS THAT WE KEEP   231

strewn haphazardly across the floor. Even my bathroom looks like a frat party happened in there.

Speechless, I walk to my now destroyed bed, crouch down, and look for what I already know isn't there.

"It's gone," I whisper, letting the angry, broken tears fall down my cheeks. "I knew that's what he was looking for."

I slump down to the floor. I don't care anymore. I don't care if they know about the adoption, or the black mail. I don't care if they see me vulnerable and weak. My eyes close as tears continue to roll down my cheeks like twin waterfalls.

"You guys should go. They got what they came for," I choke out, resting my head on the side of my bed.

A rough padded finger lightly caresses my cheekbones. Those same fingers rake through the knots in my hair as my lungs fill with the scent of cinnamon and cedar. "Shh, don't be stupid," Devon says softly. Only Dev could make the word stupid sound like a compliment. "You're not staying here tonight. We're taking you home with us."

My eyes open to a very somber looking Devon as he scoops me up from the floor and into his strong arms. "But—" I start to argue.

"Don't." The amusement is gone from Liam's voice as he comes to stand beside his brother and look me in the eye. "Don't argue. For once, just let us take care of you."

I clear my throat to do exactly what he told me not to do. "I can take care of myself," I say defiantly.

Liam, with one of my small luggage bags slung over his shoulder, lifts my bare foot in his strong hands. "Not after the damage you did to your own feet." He shakes his head and winks at me. "No shoes? Really?"

"Put me down please," I say with a sigh, rolling my eyes.

"No." Devon says nothing else as he walks toward the front door.

Once we're outside, he opens the door to the jeep and sits me down in the front passenger seat. Devon pulls the buckle down and across my chest and locks me in place.

"Devon, stop," I plead.

"No." He closes the passenger door and walks around the front to the driver's side.

The garage door begins to slide up and the rear lights give the small concrete space a red glow. I didn't notice until now, but Liam never walked out with us. He must have stayed inside and locked things up behind us before going to get Donna. How do these two men know me so well that they'd think to bring Donna with us?

New tears begin to fall as Devon pulls out of my driveway and heads into the city.

Chapter 19

Rhyann

"Let's get you cleaned up," Devon says as he pushes his way into the luxury apartment he shares with Tate and his twin brother.

He carries me through the small entryway, past the living room that looks like it was taken from a high tech showroom with the large flat panel TV that consumes an entire wall and the LED lit coffee and end tables. The entire apartment is a bachelor's techno wet dream.

"Devon," I sigh, pushing against his chest. "Stop. Put me down, I can fucking walk."

He ignores me and heads down the long hallway, pushing a door open with his shoulder.

"Seriously, Devon. Stop." I kick my feet and wiggle my body in a futile attempt to free myself from his hold.

"Have you seen your feet?" he growls as he flips on the light.

Before I can ask what the hell he's talking about, Liam brushes past us and heads for a door I hadn't noticed on the other side of the room. My eyes were stuck on the huge four poster canopy bed with the black leather headboard, black duvet, and plush red pillows. I'm not sure whose bedroom it is, but I can see myself tangled up in the bedding with either brother. Or both.

"Water's running," Liam announces, and I can hear the rush of water echoing from the open door that Liam disappeared through. I don't have another chance to protest because Devon moves through the doorway and into what has to be the most exquisite ensuite bathroom I have ever seen.

Black granite tiles with glittering white veins cover every surface from the floor to the ceiling, and even the shower walls are black granite. The deep porcelain tub with brushed copper fixtures and carved feet is the centerpiece of the entire space. And it's filling with water and bubbles.

Devon finally sits me down on the counter between the his and hers sinks. Neither brother says a word as they both go about doing little things. Liam gathers towels and a bathmat, laying the mat out on the floor at the side of the tub and hands his brother a wet cloth. Devon bends down to one knee and props my foot on his leg.

The stinging sensation tingles throughout my entire foot. I hiss through my teeth and reflexively pull my leg back. Devon's fingers dig into my ankle, holding my leg firmly. He doesn't stop his ministrations, but he looks up at me, his eyes hooded, the corners of his mouth turned down.

"Don't," Devon warns.

Okay, I've indulged his weird, neanderthal behavior enough. I roll my eyes and push at his chest with the foot he's holding so tightly. "Let me go."

He doesn't budge, not even when I kick at him a second time. His fingers just tighten over my ankle and he continues to wash the dirt and gravel from the bottom of my foot.

"Maybe next time, you'll think twice about running down the dirt road barefoot." Liam smirks from behind him.

"Excuse me?" I gawk. "I was in my own home and had a potentially violent intruder in my house. Was I supposed to call a time out just to get my shoes on before running from him?"

THE SECRETS THAT WE KEEP   237

Devon snorts. "'Time out.'" He laughs and drops one foot to pick up the other.

"Fine." Liam smirks. "You have a point. Now will you let him finish cleaning you up so we can leave you to your bath?"

I follow Liam's gaze down to his identical twin. Devon drops my ankle and glares up at me. The scowl on his beautiful face is a dark contrast to his brother's playful smirk. I know Devon hates me. All of this, all the tender touches, are a front. He'd probably be happier if I'd been kidnapped three days ago. I blink back tears I didn't realize were forming.

"Thank you." I breathe out, my heel sliding down the length of his thigh as I pull away to stand.

"Take a bath." Devon doesn't say anything else, he just stands and walks past his brother and out of the bathroom.

"I'll leave your bag on the bed for when you're done." Liam smiles down at me. "We'll be waiting out there. Movie night," he says, laughing as he closes the door, leaving me to myself and the full bubble bath.

Chapter 20

Rhyann

I leave the bathroom and on the bed, like Devon promised, is the overnight bag with all of my clothing that was hastily packed before we left my house. The house I had moved back into barely two days ago. There's another bag on the bed as well.

I take my time dressing in a pair of red cotton shorts and a matching tank top. I chance a peek into the mystery bag and am slightly horrified by what I find. What the hell is wrong with these men? What kind of kinky fuckery are they getting themselves into?

With a mixture of curiosity and amusement, I make my way from the bedroom to the open kitchen. My arm stretches out in front of me, my fingers grasping the costume tightly. "What the fuck is this?"

Devon smirks and looks in the direction of his brother, who is building a pillow fort in the middle of the living room floor. How did I miss this? And is Liam wearing a fucking furry onesie too? Dear god, I am going to lose my fucking mind because of these men.

Tate had the nerve to bring his fiancee to my house today, get angry with me when the self-righteous, condescending bitch acts like she's entitled to be in my home, and now he's standing in the kitchen, holding several boxes of pizza in his arms and smiling at me. My fists itch to connect with that perfect, gleaming white smile.

"Why aren't you wearing yours?" he asks, setting the pizza on the counter.

"Why are you here?" I ask in response.

"Movie night!" Liam exclaims, his arms outstretched, showing off his costume. He's covered from head to toe in brown fleece, a tan oval covering the front midsection of the onesie.

"What is wrong with your brother? Was he not loved enough as a child?" I look to Devon, who snorts, covering his mouth to contain his laughter.

"It's a teddy bear, Rhyann!" The genuine delight in his tone makes it hard for me to be angry with Liam.

I roll my eyes. I'm not giving in. No matter how ridiculous Liam looks, or how sweet he is, I need to stand my ground. I need to put distance between us. For the both of us. If I've learned anything lately, I've learned that I am nothing more to these men than a memory they're struggling to let go of.

"So where's Aubree?" I ask Tate, not even concerned with hiding the sneer on my face or the disdain in my voice. I don't like her, and I won't pretend to like her.

"She's having dinner with her family and an old college friend tonight." Tate answers as if it's an everyday question, like she's been a part of our little group for years.

"Why aren't you with her?"

"Would that make you happy, Rhyann?" Tate's voice is low and laced with something dark that I can't put my finger on. He glares at me, challenging me to answer his question.

My first thoughts are to say *Yes, Tate, get the fuck out of here and my life for good.* But then there's a part of me that hurts, that aches like I'm being stabbed by a searing hot knife, when I think about never seeing Tate again, never smelling his cologne or hearing his laugh.

The tension in the room is so thick, it's hard to breathe. I don't even notice the twins leaving us.

"One last movie night?" Tate asks softly, his expression shifting from one of anger to something resembling sadness or longing.

Movie nights were our thing as kids. It was the only time we stopped bickering or picking on each other and were friends. True friends. But so much has changed since then. We aren't the kids we were when we started our movie nights. The teenagers who fought hard to keep the tradition going are long gone.

We've grown up, become adults. We are shadows of the people we thought we'd become. "Why?" I can't help but ask, my voice laced with emotions that mirror the look in Tate's eyes.

"Because, I fucked everything up, Rhyann." Tate closes the distance between us. "Because after tonight, I won't have this chance with you ever again. And I don't know if I can handle that."

I open my mouth to say something, to ask him what he means. But I'm afraid I won't like the answer. Before I can get the words out, he nods to the onesie in my hand and changes the subject completely. "Liam bought that for you. Said it's an apology for being a dick today. I told him that just breathing the same air as you makes him a dick."

He laughs at his own joke and brushes past me to join his two best friends. His fingers lightly touch my hand as he passes and it takes all my strength not to grab him and make him stay, beg him to explain, to choose me over Aubree. But he was never mine to begin with, and even if there was a chance, I likely ruined it by sleeping with his best friends. If only he knew, maybe then things would be easier for us.

Chapter 21

I'm impressed when Rhyann comes out of the room a few minutes later. I didn't know what changed, her mind or her attitude, but she walks out wearing that god-awful onesie Liam bought her.

"Well, look at you. Playing nice for once." I smirk as she pulls a bottle of vino out of the wine fridge under the wet bar on the far side of the room.

"Oh, eat shit and die, Tate." She rolls her eyes, pouring herself a glass of wine.

"Are you going to pour me a glass?" I wouldn't say I like wine. I rarely drink at all, if I'm being honest. But the idea of her hating me is easier to bear than breaking her heart.

She takes a very impolite swig of the wine, then spits it back in the delicate clear glass and sets it on the coffee table in front of me. "You know what, here. Have this one."

I can't hold back my laughter as she swipes the open bottle off the counter, takes the bowl of popcorn in front of me, and walks to the other side of the living room. Guess I'm drinking a glass of wine tonight.

I take my wine and settle in on one end of the massive couch. Rhyann grabs a throw blanket and gets comfortable on the other end. The sofa is deep and well-tufted. It's the perfect movie night couch.

"What are we watching?" Liam asks from a pillow mountain on the floor. I'm not sure how much he actually grew over the years. Mentally speaking. Physically, the man is a mountain, but there are moments when his brother and I can't help but wonder if he thinks he's still a kid.

"I need more wine," Rhyann declares, standing up empty-handed and walking out of the room.

"The Revenant?" Dev suggests.

Liam groans. "How many times have you seen that movie?"

"Too many." I cough into my hand.

"What does the princess want to watch?" Liam asks.

Rhyann returns, having switched her wine for a whiskey tumbler of amber liquid. I quirk my brow at her.

She shrugs. "If I'm stuck with you ass hats, we're watching The Purge. Maybe it'll give me creative ideas."

"What are you drinking, princess?" Liam slides in between Rhyann and me as she sits down on her end of the couch. "Didn't like your wine?"

"I finished the wine. I need something stronger to get through this movie night."

"That whole bottle?" Liam's tone is a mix of fear and awe.

"Don't look at me like that, Liam. Trust me, if you guys didn't insist on tormenting me, I would have had one glass, read a couple chapters of a book, and gone to sleep."

"No judgment, princess. I would have joined you if I knew you liked the good stuff!" Liam hops up and walks toward the kitchen.

I look at Rhyann over the rim of the wine glass. I wink as I take a sip. "Be careful. She spits in the booze."

DEVON

Rhyann passes out before the movie even gets to the good part, the part where the masked people force their way into the family's home. She looks so small, curled up on the arm of the couch, taking up as little space as possible.

She refused to sit anywhere near me, my brother, or Tate. She really does hate us and wants us out of her life. A small part of me feels guilty, but another small part of me enjoys it. I need it; my body craves her hatred like I crave water or air. It keeps my head clear, keeps me from making mistakes that I can't bear to make with her.

After the movie ends, Liam and Tate put the pillows back on the sofa and chairs in the room while I go around and gather the empty plates and glasses. We argue a little over who is giving up their bed for her, and I refuse to back down. Tate has her heart, he always has and he always will. Even if neither of them will acknowledge it.

THE SECRETS THAT WE KEEP

My brother has her body. It's only right that I get to keep her safe.

He assumes I thought his fling with her years ago was over, but I know better. He's my twin for fuck's sake. I knew she was his first love; the problem was, she was mine too, and even though I'd die for my twin, I wanted her, so I took her. Then I hurt her, because that's what I do, that's who I am. Where Liam is light and warm, there's nothing but dark and cold in me.

The guys don't fight me much on this, and they leave me to my task. She's warm and light as a feather when I lift her sleeping body and cradle her against my chest. On instinct, she stretches and wraps her arms around my neck. The fiery sweet scent of vanilla and cinnamon fills my lungs, and I let out a low groan.

"Bro, I told you I'd take her to bed if you're not strong enough to lift her."

I turn and growl at my twin before walking down the hall. He may be my brother, and Tate may be my best friend. We all have a spot in our hearts for Rhyann, but I'll be damned if I'm going to allow anyone to carry her when she's vulnerable and defenseless.

It isn't that I don't trust them, it's just...

It's Rhyann. We spent years protecting her from the world, from herself. She deserves better than us. She deserves better than the senseless fear and loneliness I know she's feeling.

A sigh escapes my lips, blowing a few strands of hair across her forehead. She responds to the soft whoosh by burrowing her face further into my embrace. Fuck. What is wrong with me? This is the one person in the whole world I can never have. The one person who's off limits to all three of us.

My bedroom already has all her belongings in it, so it was an easy argument to win. The room is clean. There's no ostentatious bed to take up space. It's simple, big enough for two. A black velvet tufted headboard backing up a couple of pillows, nothing flouncy or decorative. The duvet matches the color scheme. Black and gold and white.

I set her down on the bed and pull the opposite side of the duvet over her body, folding her petite form between the layers.

"I know what you're thinking about, man," my brother breaks the silence behind me.

"I highly doubt that."

THE SECRETS THAT WE KEEP 249

He laughs. "She's something special. What do you think she'd do if she caught you watching her sleep?"

My brother's endearing love for her is nothing like what I feel for her. It's everything she deserves in this world. The security, the protection, the devotion.

"She'd probably kick you right in the nose and break it all over again," Tate laughs from the doorway.

I smile, remembering the first time my nose was broken. She kissed me, and I kissed her back. It was incredible. We were young, I was fifteen and she was thirteen. But Tate, Liam, and I had all agreed before then, Rhyann was off limits. The problem was, she didn't know she was off limits to us, not at first. So, when Tate found out about the kiss, rather than let him be angry with her, I took the blame. I told him and everyone else I forced her to kiss me, that I pinned her down in the grass and took what didn't belong to me.

So, Tate kicked my ass. Broke my nose, and then helped me get home so my parents could take me to the doctor to have it set right. My mother said I got what I deserved, that I should never have forced myself on a girl. My sister was disgusted with me; she saw Rhyann almost as a sister. But Liam. He knew, he knew that every dirty look, every whispered bit of disdain I got for the next three months, it was all worth it for her.

"Let her sleep, man. She's safe here, with us right on the other side of the door." Liam interrupts my reminiscing with a strong hand on my shoulder. "Besides, you hate her, and she hates you. Remember?"

He has a point, and a part of me wants, needs her to hate me. To remind me who and what I am. They never found the guys who raped my sister because I made sure there were no bodies left to find. The same will go for whoever's trying to hurt Rhyann.

Liam and Tate are the only ones who know almost everything, who know most of my darkest secrets. The things that I keep hidden in the shadows away from others. They know the depravity I'm capable of.

"Yeah. You sure the security system is good?"

If looks could kill, I'd be dead. Liam glares at me with a fire in his eyes that could turn a man to ashes. "You doubt my work? After all these years?"

"Nah. But I don't trust whoever's been fucking with her not try something." I let out a breath as I turn out the lights and leave her room.

"How would they know to find her here?"

Another good point, but... "Someone was able to get past your system at her house. Who's to say they won't here?"

"If they do, they'll have to get through us first," Tate says, his voice tainted with carefully controlled rage.

I called him on the way here, told him what happened at Rhyann's house. He left his fiancee with her family and made his way here. He's a fucking fool if he doesn't see what she does to him. Tonight was the second time he left Aubree for Rhyann. I don't understand why he's marrying the girl, but I won't fight him on it. I just hope he doesn't hurt Rhy. If he does, it won't be only his nose being broken.

Chapter 22

Rhyann

It's dark when I pry my eyes open. The room spins slowly like a children's teacup ride at a carnival, and I can feel the remnants of my last meal attempting to make an appearance. Fuck, why did I drink so much? I roll over and pull the soft blanket further up my arms.

The jostling of my body invokes a violent tumbling in my stomach. "Oh god," I whisper into the darkness and bury my face into the soft, fluffy pillow.

The spicy scents of cinnamon and clove, mixed with a little bit of citrus, overtake my senses. The pillow smells so much like Devon that I moan.

"Shh," a deep voice says in the darkness. "Drink some water."

Soft fingers caress my cheek and lift my head so my lips can meet the hard glass. As the tepid water slowly presses past my dry lips, the male voice continues to make soothing sounds while combing his fingers through my knotted hair.

"That's it, sweet Ginger," he says softly, pulling the glass from my lips. "Now sleep." He coaxes me gently back down and under the covers.

I wake with the worst headache. At first, I'm not sure where I am, then I remember the night before, and the whiskey I downed.

"Fuck," I moan, looking around.

There's a glass of water on the nightstand. There's also a bottle of ibuprofen and a small glass of a greenish liquid. What the hell? Picking up the glass I bring it to my nose and sniff. The briny, tangy scent hits me and I smile. Pickle juice. The perfect hangover cure.

I quickly down the green liquid, toss a couple ibuprofen in my mouth, and finish off the glass of water. My ears ring as I push off the bed and stand. I let out a moan and press the heels of my hands into my temples.

After a quick shower, and some searching for my clothes, I make my way out of the bedroom and into the large living room. I expect to find your typical post pizza night scene, empty boxes and plates, beer bottles and soda cans all over the place. But no, the entire place is clean, spotless. There's not even a single throw pillow out of place.

"Good morning, princess," Liam calls from the kitchen.

Seated at the counter sipping coffee are Liam, Devon, and Tate. I let out a frustrated groan. "What are you doing here?"

All three men laugh sarcastically. "Aside from the fact that I live here?" Tate offers with a quirked brow. "I wanted to make sure you were feeling okay, and offer you a ride into the office."

The bitter, "For now," from Devon didn't go unmissed. I give him a questioning look but he refuses to meet my eyes.

From the second he told me about Aubree, Devon hasn't hidden his disdain for her. I can't blame him. She's poison dressed in a candy wrapper.

Last night over the billiards table, I finally realized why Aubree seemed familiar to me. I think back to my years at Evangeline's and laugh to myself. Aubree either doesn't recognize me or she's playing some kind of mind game. My bet is on the latter.

Aubree was the reigning queen of manipulation and mind games at Evangeline's. I was two grades ahead of her, but she'd been going there since elementary school, and she pretty much ruled the entire student body. The minute I arrived in the dorm rooms, she made it her life's mission to make sure I knew I was not welcome in her school.

"Be right back." Tate stands from his spot at the counter, pulling his phone from his pocket.

I can see him lifting it to his ear as he walks down the hallway opposite of the room I slept in the night before. I can't hear what he is saying to the person on the other end, but his back goes rigid seconds after answering it. Unsure of what that's about, I turn back to the twins.

"Devon, you didn't have to give up your bed for me."

Rather than respond, he slides a tall mug filled with black coffee over to me. I prefer my coffee black, and I'm pleasantly surprised that he remembers that. I offer a genuine smile and take the first sip of the hot liquid.

"So, what's on the agenda today, princess?" Liam asks with a smile, his knee swinging softly into the side of my leg. "Wanna shirk our responsibilities and go hide out on the coast for the day?"

I open my mouth the answer, but before I can Devon speaks up. "Why in the fuck would she want to do that?" he asks. "And with you?"

Liam laughs, and I use the coffee mug to hide my smile. The entire conversation from here goes so smoothly, it's almost like we've been doing this for years. There's a warm feeling forming inside my chest, and I don't think it's from the coffee.

"Thank you for taking care of me last night," I say softly to Devon.

He nods in response just as Tate walks back into the kitchen. "Sorry, guys. I have to go pick Aubree up and take her into the city," Tate explains with an exacerbated look. "She's having some wedding plans crisis and it's something that she apparently needs me for."

"Whatever. Just don't forget, we have a meeting with the city about the club today at eleven," Devon reminds his best friend.

"We should be done by then, man," Tate says, walking toward the front of the apartment. "Aubree wants to be a big part of the club anyway, so I promised her she can join us today." Without a response from Devon, Tate walks out the door.

THE SECRETS THAT WE KEEP   257

"I really don't like his fiancee," Liam breaks the awkward silence, and I can't help but give him the biggest smile. "I knew it! You don't like her either, princess."

"What gave that away?" I ask with a smirk.

"It doesn't matter," Devon interrupts. "Tate loves her, so we have to put up with her." He gives me a pointed look as if he was talking directly to me. "Now that you're up and about, I'm going to go shower. Then we can discuss your plans for the day." His expression is dark. I know he hates me, has hated me for years, but lately it seems like he almost cares.

As Devon walks past me, I follow him out, grabbing his bicep just before he goes down the hall to his bedroom. "Dev, wait."

Before I can breathe out another word, he has my back pinned against the wall, his nose caressing the soft skin of my earlobe. "Care to join me, princess?" he asks, a growl in his throat. "The shower's big enough for the both of us. Or would you prefer I was my playful and sweet brother?"

"Stop being a dick." I push off the wall behind me, but with his arm across my chest, I'm stuck. "I just wanted to thank you for the water and medicine for my hangover, and for being there last night."

He laughs, his arm not wavering, keeping me in place. "That's some steamy dream you had, princess." His knee pushes between my legs, his strong chest sandwiching me in. "If I were in that bedroom with you last night, I'd have crawled into bed with you." He catches the tender flesh of my earlobe between his teeth. "Trust me, *princess*, you were all alone last night. We gave you exactly what you asked for."

The way he calls me princess feels like he's spraying acid at me, every syllable filled with vitriol. I know he was in there. I know someone was in there with me. "Whatever, let me go, Devon." I push at him.

His arm slowly slides down my chest, brushing against my hard nipples to rest against my belly. "Maybe you were dreaming about my brother," he laughs. "Or Tate?" His voice is husky and low. Strong fingers slip beneath the hem of my black satin blouse and begin tracing tiny circles over the soft skin.

"Devon," I whisper. "Please let me go."

Hot lips press against the pulse point on my neck. "You see, Rhyann. I can't do that." His voice is sad, pained by something unseen, a drastic contrast to the hatred coming from him moments ago. I'm so wrapped up in

THE SECRETS THAT WE KEEP

the sorrow behind them, I barely catch his words. "You belong to me. You always have and you always will."

Before I can respond, before I have the opportunity to argue with him, his lips smash against mine in a searing, hard kiss.

My body ignores my mental commands to fight him, to push him away from me. Instead, my lips part and I let out a breathy moan. He takes the opportunity and slips his tongue between my teeth, teasing and tangling with my tongue.

The velvety soft muscle creates a languid dance in my mouth. A dance I can feel all the way down to my core.

I lean into the kiss, pressing myself against Devon's body. His knee spreads my denim-clad legs wider, opening me for him to devour the lingering space between us. His arm against my stomach keeps my back pinned to the wall while his free hand flicks the buttons at my waist open.

Those same fingers push their way past the loosened waistband of my jeans, past the lace hem of my panties. Before my mind can register what he's doing, I find myself moaning against his lips while his fingers play with my clit, mimicking the motion of his tongue in my mouth.

"Devon," I moan.

His lips stretch into a smile against my mouth. "God, I love the way you say my name, princess."

"Why are you doing this?" I ask as the onslaught in my pants continues. My body betrays my words, however, as I grind my core into his hand, seeking deeper friction. Fuck. I want him. I don't know why I want him. I can't explain this driving need; maybe it's the lack of sex this past year.

"Because you're mine, and I can do what I want with you."

His reply is so simple, so matter of fact, I have to consciously refrain from nodding my head in agreement.

"No," I force myself to say. "I don't belong to anyone."

The hand that had been holding me to the wall slides from my waist to my thigh. Devon traces the tattoo he knows is inked into my skin. "Is that so?"

His chest pushes me flush against the wall and his hands continue their sweet torture. "Mmmhmm." I nod my head, my bottom lip trapped between my teeth to keep the trembling from betraying me.

"Then tell me, why is my artwork inked on your thigh?"

Shit. I should have known this would come up at some point. His reaction to the tattoo the other night rocked me. I never thought Devon would remember drawing such a simple picture all those years ago.

"It was pretty," I lie. How do I tell him that that picture, the one he drew for me the day of my father's funeral, has been a symbol of strength and hope to me ever since. That I had it tattooed so it's always with me, so the boy I gave my heart to years ago is with me.

"Bullshit," he growls. The hand that's been slowly teasing my nether regions is yanked from my pants and he grips my chin. I can feel my own wetness on the tips of his fingers as he forces me to look into his icy blue eyes. "This, right here. It means you're mine. You've been mine since the day I met you, and you'll be mine until the day you die." His hand tightens around my thigh, and he kisses me forcefully before opening the bedroom door and pulling me in with him.

I stop dead in my tracks when my eyes catch sight of the display by the window. I hadn't noticed it when I got up this morning, or after I showered and dressed. If I had, I would have screamed, bringing all three men to the room sooner.

"Oh my god," I breathe out, holding back the bile rising in my throat.

Chapter 23

Liam

"Liam!" Dev yells from across the apartment. I'm not sure what's going on between him and Rhyann right now, and I do know they have history, but this is not his "Hey bro, wanna join us?" tone. Not that we've ever shared a woman before.

"What's up?" I ask as I make my way down the short hallway to Devon's room. Standing at the threshold is Rhyann. She's staring at something in the room, arms folded, her fingers gripping the backs of her forearms.

What she's staring at so intensely is something out of a horror movie. The drapes covering the large window on the far side of the wall are covered in dark red—god, I hope that's not blood— writing. The words *See You Soon Ginger* are painted on them.

"Did you set the alarm and lock the doors last night?" My brother's words are slow, controlled. I've only seen this level of rage in his eyes once in my life.

"Fuck, of course I did. Who would do this?" I rake my fingers through my hair as I come to stand next to Rhyann. I wrap my arm around her shaking shoulders and pull her into me.

"I told you I wasn't alone in here last night," she whispers.

"This wasn't done last night. It's fresh," Devon says, running his finger down one of the letters. "It's paint." He wipes the red off on one of the few dry spots on the drapes and walks toward me and Rhyann.

"I want to see the security footage," he growls. "For the entire building."

"No one should have been able to get into our apartment. Not without a key or the door codes," I remind my brother.

"Exactly, and there are only three people who know any of those things." Devon looks at Rhyann. "What exactly happened last night?"

"I woke up, couldn't remember where I was for a minute, then I saw you," she starts.

"Wasn't me."

"Right," she sighs and continues. "Whoever it was, he handed me the glass of water, told me to drink, and called me Ginger." Rhyann looks over at the nightstand where an empty glass and bottle of ibuprofen are sitting. "I should have known it wasn't you when he called me Ginger. No one except my father ever called me that."

As Rhyann talks, she begins to shake more, and I can see the tears welling up in her eyes. On instinct, I pull her into my chest and wrap her in a tight embrace. My fingers rake over her back as I slowly guide her out of the room.

"We need to call the detectives," Devon offers, following behind us.

"No," Rhy speaks up.

I get her settled on the couch before I go get my laptop from my own bedroom and return, pulling up the security feed from last night.

"Why not?" Devon asks.

Rhyann clears her throat before she says the words that blow a hole through both mine and my brother's souls. "I think Tate and Adrian have something to do with all this."

"No," I say. "He wouldn't, they wouldn't do anything to hurt you, Rhyann."

Devon, who's been pacing back and forth since he walked out of his bedroom, turns to me. His blue eyes are dark with rage and the need to hurt someone or something. I know that look all too well. I know his pain as if it were my own. Sometimes, growing up, it felt like it was my own, so I tried even harder to always be happy and find the bright side of things.

"I think she's right," he finally says.

"Absolutely not," I defend our best friend. "He would never do anything to hurt Rhyann, and he wouldn't betray us."

Devon looks at Rhyann. That's the only time his features soften. There's never been a secret between us, except for whatever happened between the two of them. I knew when we were kids, he fell head over heels in love with her. He told me about the time they were secretly dating because Tate told us she was off limits, and he told me when it ended. He never said why, but when I caught up with Rhyann after her grandfather's funeral, all she would say was that they hated each other and she couldn't care less if she ever saw my twin brother again. The look he's been giving her since she came home is not the look you give someone you hate.

"He was there when the person tried to kidnap me at my apartment," Rhyann says, finally breaking the silence. "Yesterday, I met with the lawyer. Found out that Adrian's been lying to me."

"About?" Devon asks, stopping in front of her.

"I could have taken over Devereux Publications immediately following my graduation. I don't have to wait until I'm twenty-five. Why would he try to keep me from my own company?" Her question comes out on the tail of a sob.

"Didn't Aubree say something the other night about Devereux becoming hers and Tate's?" Devon asks.

I still don't believe it. "That's just the wishful ramblings of a vapid, self centered, spoiled debutant. I'd listen to a seal bark before I listened to her."

"The stuff that was stolen last night was everything the lawyer gave me about my inheritance and my adoption," Rhyann says to no one in particular.

I give their words some thought. Not missing the confession she just made, I turn to Rhyann, resting my hand on her knee. "Hey, look at me, princess."

When she looks at me, her green eyes are swimming in pools of tears waiting to fall. It shreds my heart to see her hurt like this. She's known more pain in her life than any person should ever experience. "My grandfather was getting threatening emails, right before he died," she tells us. "They were threatening to expose my adoption. Expose me as not being the heir to Devereux."

"The detectives are on their way now," Devon says before dropping to his knees in front of Rhyann. "Look at me, princess."

I gain access to the building camera feed within minutes. As the owner of the company who set up their security system, I have a key code that allows me access in an emergency situation. This might not count for an emergency as far as the building owners are concerned, but fuck them. They'll end up granting the detectives access later anyway.

My brother and Rhyann are quiet beside me as I work. Before I look at the CCTV footage, I pull up the private security footage for our apartment. There's a camera outside the door, and two inside the main living space. One of them faces the entry way, and the other faces the patio door leading to the balcony. Tate said it was pointless to have the cameras inside, especially the one facing the patio, seeing as we are five stories up, but the more angles today, the better.

The first camera, the one outside, shows us arriving with Rhyann, and twenty minutes later Tate comes home. Everything seems normal on the outside, so I switch to the inside feed. Same thing. I fast forward a while, watch as I lock the doors and arm the alarm system. Then everything goes dark. Nothing. If our apartment cameras show nothing, it's not likely the buildings cameras will either. I have a sinking feeling in my gut as I close the laptop and look at my brother and the only girl I've ever loved.

"Say Tate did this," I start. "What are we supposed to do? Why would he want to hurt Rhyann?"

Devon looks at me with the most "Isn't it obvious?" expression on his face. But it's Rhyann who answers me.

"I think Adrian wants Devereux. He and my grandfather had some kind of secret romance after my father died and his wife left. What if he thinks it should be his, not mine?"

"Didn't you tell me that the detectives gave Adrian the toxicology results for the wine from the other night?" Devon tacks on. He has a point, and Rhyann's reasoning makes sense.

"Wait, him and your grandfather?" I ask, circling back to that giant secret that the older man took to his grave with him.

"Is there a problem with that?" my brother asks defensively.

I give him a look with my brows raised. He knows I am not judgemental, and would never deny anyone their right to love who they want. "No, I'm just surprised is all. The old man was Adrian's best friend's dad."

There's a knock at the door, and I look at my laptop to pull up the live feed. The footage from the night before continued to run, and what's playing now is about six hours after Tate arrived home.

"I'll get the door," Devon says in an annoyed tone.

On the screen, a tall frame in baggy clothes and a black hoodie with the hood pulled all the way over their head is at the door. He punches in the code to unlock the door, and slips inside. I can't believe what I'm seeing right now. I hit pause on the outside feed and switch to the camera facing the inside entryway.

At the same time stamp, the same figure slips into the apartment, closing the door behind him. It's as though he knows where the camera is, and he angles his body so that his face is obstructed the entire time. I watch, speechless, as the intruder disarms the alarm system and uses the private codes to shut off the security feeds. The feed picks back up this morning, minutes before Tate left, the same figure from the night before quietly slipping through the door after resetting the system.

Someone knows our codes, our cameras, and our weaknesses. This is bad, this is very bad.

The detectives take pictures of Devon's room, and dust damned near every inch of the house for fingerprints. They check both mine and Tate's rooms as well. A small amount of guilt nags at the back of my mind for lying to the detectives and telling them we had permission to enter Tate's room, but what else was I supposed to do? He wasn't answering his phone, and Rhyann and Devon both want to keep him and Adrian out of this until they know more.

Devon explains his theory to the detectives. He tells them everything Rhyann told us, and how it wasn't until they mentioned it that we were made aware of the test results. They agreed that keeping Tate and his father out of the loop for now is the best thing, as well as informing us of a charity gala Adrian is hosting tonight. In honor of his son's new fiancee.

The three of us sit in the living room. Devon is in his usual spot in the wing backed, leather chair near the patio doors, and Rhyann and I occupy separate ends of the couch. "Well, I know what we're doing tonight," Devon says, looking at his phone after the detectives leave.

"I still need to go into the office," Rhyann speaks up.

I wish she would let this go for now. Stay with us, let us keep her safe. "Princess, I really don't think—"

"I think it's exactly what she should do, brother," Devon cuts me off. "Think about it, if she goes in, she'll have Adrian thinking she isn't afraid of these sick games. I think all three of us need to play it off like nothing has changed. Nothing's happened today."

What he says makes sense on the logical level. "But, Rhyann. What about her safety?" I ask, looking from my brother to Rhyann. Neither of them seem all that concerned for her safety. "How are we supposed to keep her safe, and still go on like nothing happened?"

"I'm going with her," Devon says, matter of factly.

"No, you're not!" The shock on Rhyann's face when she argues Devon's plan puts a smile on my face. She'd been so quiet and detached while the detectives were here that I worried she was shutting down like she did when her grandfather died.

"Yes, I am," Devon growls at her. "Do not fight us on this."

Rhyann stands up and stalks toward my brother. What I wouldn't give for a giant soda and a bucket of popcorn right now. At her full height, she stands maybe five foot five, with her heels on. The fight that's been brewing between the two of them will be one worthy of a pay-per-view special.

"No, you are not," she says, standing toe to toe with my brother. "I don't need a babysitter."

Devon closes the space between them. "I'm not a fucking babysitter, princess." He wraps his arm around her neck, his fingers tangling in her fiery red hair. "I keep my things safe, and we've already gone over this. You're mine."

"Ours," I chime in, crossing one leg over the other knee. We've both known for years that it would come to this one day. Both of us love her, both of us want her. We've never shared a woman before, but we've never had an interest in anyone but Rhyann. We don't have to discuss it to know that if she'll have us both, we will happily share her.

"Excuse me?" Rhyann attempts to turn and glare at me. I can hear the anger in her voice. Or is it shock, disgust maybe? Devon keeps her still, staring down into her eyes.

"I won't lose you too, Rhyann," his voice is soft, his words slow. I watch the two of them, pride welling up in my chest at the hope that my brother might finally open up, just a little, about his fears and feelings. "Neither one of us can handle another loss."

"I. Am. Not. Property." she says through gritted teeth.

With a sigh, I stand and make my way to the two of them. They're both like raging storms on the ocean. Both set for destruction, both on the same path. I worry that if I don't intervene now, they'll push each other farther away than they already have.

"Rhy, please," I plead, coming up behind her. "Let us keep you safe. Let Devon keep you safe today."

My brother releases Rhyann's hair from his grip, but continues to cup her neck. She's so small compared to us. I glance at my brother over her head. His face is stoic, void of emotion, but I can see the sorrow and fear swirling in his eyes.

"I'm not Gemma," Rhyann says, tears falling down her cheeks like a rainstorm against a window pane. "I don't need to be saved."

The mention of our sister sends a knife into both mine and Devon's hearts. It's a low blow, even for Rhyann. Especially for Rhyann. It's true, she wasn't here when Gemma died, she didn't see what it did to us, to our family, but out of anyone, she knows the devastating pain of losing a part of you better than anyone I know.

"No. You aren't her," Devon grinds out. "She wouldn't have intentionally put herself in danger." He drops his hands and storms off in the direction of his room.

"Devon," Rhyann cries out behind him.

"Rhy, let him do this please," I ask, turning her to face me as I wrap her in my arms.

"I'm sorry," she sobs into my chest. "I'm so frustrated, and scared. I feel helpless and lied to. I didn't mean to—"

"Shh, it's okay." I kiss the top of her head. "Just let him do this. He loves you, he needs you."

"No, he doesn't." She shakes her head. "He hates me, he just loves torturing me."

I groan. My brother has made a mess of his relationship with Rhyann. His jealousy complicates so much of his life. There are things I wish I could tell her. Things only I know about my brother that would explain so much. But they aren't my secrets to share. "Go to him, Rhyann," I encourage her. "He needs you."

I can feel the shift in her emotions as she pulls out of my embrace. "What the fuck?" she seethes, the fear and sadness gone from her eyes. "I'm not just some kind of fuck toy for you and Devon to pass around."

"No one ever said you were."

She stares up at me, balling her fists at her sides, rage written across her features. "Then what the fuck are you implying? Because I'd rather take my chances with this stalker slash kidnapper than be yours and Devon's whore to be passed around and tossed out when you're finished with me."

"Oh princess," I moan, grabbing onto Rhyann's hand and pulling her into my arms. "You were always end game for us. Didn't you know?"

"I don't get it." She looks up at me, calm starting to settle over her beautiful features.

"Devon and I are two halves of one whole. Is it that much of a surprise that we fell in love with the same woman?" I ask, brushing a renegade strand of hair from her face.

THE SECRETS THAT WE KEEP

"He hates me, Liam," she says. "He took my virginity, stole my heart out of spite. Then he left me for some girl you guys went to school with."

I knew all of this already. I also knew what he did, when he did it, wasn't out of love, but out of jealousy. He saw how close she and Tate were starting to become, and he couldn't take either of them being close without him. My brother is all kinds of complicated, and I think I'm the only one who's ever understood him.

"No, he doesn't hate you, Rhyann. He hates himself."

She stares up at me, her face tear streaked, her eyes glistening with a new well of tears waiting to spill. "What are you asking me to do, Liam?"

There's the million dollar question that I don't think I even know the answer to. "I don't know, baby. I just know that we can't go on without you, and as much as I want to climb into my bed with you and hide until all this is settled, it's my brother who needs you right now."

"I don't know..." Rhyann sighs into my chest, wrapping her arms around my waist and holding on tightly.

"Hey." I tip her chin up and look into her sea green eyes. "Just go to him, talk to him. Assure him that everything will be okay. He's scared right now." We both are, but I don't tell her that.

She nods her head and lets go of me. It feels like I'm sending a lamb to slaughter. The mixture of fear, longing, and heartbreak screams at me from behind her eyes. I lace my fingers with hers and lead her down the hall to my brother's door.

"Go, it's fine. He needs you, and I need you both. I'll think of a game plan for tonight while the two of you talk."

I open the door for her. She gives me a sad smile and nods before disappearing behind the white painted wood.

Chapter 24

Rhyann

"Devon," I call out. I look everywhere in the room, except at the window and the message painted there. I can hear the shower running in the adjoining bathroom. The door's open a crack.

I can't do this. What the fuck kind of game is this? Liam isn't the type to play with my emotions. But Devon, he has always enjoyed seeing me uncomfortable, and Liam would do anything for his twin.

I turn back to the door and open it. Liam leans against the wall, his arms folded and a sad expression on his face. "I knew you'd turn around immediately," he admits. "It's okay, Rhyann."

I fight the tears that threaten to fall. My heart is beating so hard, I'm afraid it's going to rip right out of my chest. Maybe it should. The pain of that would be less than what I'm feeling right now. "This is so fucked up, Liam."

"Why?" he asks, caressing my cheek. "We know you love us both, and we love you. What's so fucked up about that?"

The vulnerability and love I see in his eyes has me second guessing all of my decisions in the past. He's right, I do love them both. I've loved all three boys for as long as I can remember. I just always thought one day I'd either have to choose one or choose none of them. Right here, right now, Liam is giving me a third option.

"It'll never work," I say. "He won't want this."

"I can hear you," Devon yells from the bathroom.

"Go and find out." Liam kisses me softly. "I'll be figuring out what to do about our best friend problem while you two are working things out." He kisses me one last time before closing the door with a wink.

Hesitantly, I make my way to the bathroom. The water isn't running in the background anymore, and I hear the clank of the shower door closing before I look inside. Nothing could prepare me for the breathtaking sight I find when I finally open the door.

"What do you want?" Devon asks, wrapping a fluffy black towel around his waist.

"Dev," I start. He looks up at me. His black hair is glistening and pushed back from his face. I'm knocked

THE SECRETS THAT WE KEEP

breathless when his eyes collide with mine. The ice in his stare has melted to reveal a stormy blue so stunning I can't form words. "I—"

He doesn't wait for me to move, or speak. Before I can clear my mind, I'm swept up in his arms, his hot full mouth covering mine in the most intense kiss I've ever experienced.

"The minute you walked through that door, you agreed to be mine, I hope you know that," he says against my lips as he lifts me up, wrapping my legs around his waist.

Deep down, I know he's right. I knew that when I opened the door a few minutes ago to find Liam waiting for me. I knew when I was a teenager, and gave Devon my virginity, that he was always going to be it for me. I just needed someone to hate, to be hated by. Devon gave me everything I needed. Why I never saw it until now, I don't know, but I hope it isn't too late.

"I've always been yours," I whisper against his lips.

"It's about goddamn time," he growls, setting me down on the bathroom counter. As soon as my ass hits the cold marble, Devon releases me and begins a hurried attempt to unfasten my jeans.

My fingers shake as I take over. He watches me the entire time, his eyes not leaving mine as he lifts one foot then the other, removing my boots with ease. His hands move up my calves and over my thighs. He grips the waistband of my jeans and slips them down, taking my lace panties with them, dropping them to the floor in a heap below me.

"God, I've missed you," Devon breathes, running a finger down the side of my face. "I wish I had more time to savor this moment, but you have a company to take over."

The sinister smile on his face when he says those words would scare anyone else off. Me? They turn me on. I reach out and pull at the towel covering Devon's waist. It falls with ease, joining my pants on the floor.

I suck in a breath when my eyes land on Devon's hard cock. Holy shit, I'd forgotten how big he is. I smile, wondering if he and Liam have ever compared penis sizes. I might have to find out sometime. I hold back my laugh at the images my mind conjures of the two of them comparing dick sizes.

"What's so funny?" Devon growls, fisting his cock.

THE SECRETS THAT WE KEEP   283

Oops. In my attempt to stifle my horribly timed sense of humor, I snorted. "Nothing," I say, wrapping my legs around his waist, pulling him and his dick closer to me.

"Nuh uh." Devon puts his empty hand between us. "Tell me what you were thinking about, or I'll take care of myself and force you to watch."

"It's nothing, I swear." The asshole would absolutely do what he's threatening to do. "I was just thinking about something Liam said."

"You're thinking about my brother while staring at my cock?" He arches an eyebrow, the corner of his mouth twitching in amusement.

"I was wondering—it's stupid, never mind." My cheeks heat with embarrassment.

Devon lines the head of his cock up with my wet pussy and slides the slick tip up and down the seam between my folds. "No, tell me," he commands. "Or else this is how we will sit until I cum in my own hand."

I let out a moan. I've never felt so empty, so needy as I do right now. With a sigh, I bite my lip and look into his blue eyes. "Please," I beg, scooting further out on the counter, pressing his cock closer into me. A whimper escapes my throat when I'm denied his dick.

"What were you thinking, princess?" he asks patiently.

"I was wondering," I began.

"Go on." Devon slips the head of his cock between my plump lips, resting it at the entrance of my core.

"I wondered if you two ever compared sizes," I blurt out before looking away. My face burns from humiliation. I can't believe I actually admitted to thinking about that.

Devon doesn't pull away, he doesn't laugh or mock me. Instead, he slams his cock deep into me. His fingers dig into my hips as he closes the distance between us, stealing my breath and wrenching another moan from my lips.

"You tell me, princess. You're the only one who's ever had both of us. Who's bigger?" he asks while pumping into me.

"Oh god, Devon," I moan. "I don't know." My hips buck to meet his rhythm.

"Do you need us both to decide?" He grunts between thrusts. "Would you like that, Rhyann? Would you like to be fucked by me and Liam at the same time?"

My breath catches in my throat and my eyes go wide when I look at Devon. He's serious. The intensity in his stare as he fucks me tells me it's something he has given serious thought to.

The idea of being filled by both of them thrills me. Picturing myself, both holes filled by both brothers at once, sends bolts of lightning between my thighs. I brace myself against the counter with one hand and slip the other between my legs. My fingers find my clit and begin rubbing little circles over the cluster of nerves.

"You would like that, wouldn't you?"

"Mmmhmm," I moan as he pumps into me.

"Tell me your fantasy, Rhyann. How would you like it?" Devon asks huskily.

"Both," I moan loudly. The muscles in my core clench around his cock. Thinking about having him and Liam has me so close to orgasm. I've never cum so fast, not even with my sex toys.

"Both what? Cocks? Holes? Which holes, you have three beautiful, perfect holes."

So. Fucking. Close. "All of it," I say. "I need you both to fuck me in all of them."

"Look at me, Rhyann." His voice is hoarse.

I open my eyes to see Devon watching me, his hips pumping between my thighs as we both reach our climax together. His back straightens and his glutes clench beneath my heels. A jolt of electricity hits my clit and it begins to pulse beneath my finger in time with Devon's cock pulsing inside me.

Chapter 25

Rhyann

Less than fifteen minutes after Liam left me in Devon's room to decide my own fate, the three of us are sitting in Donna as we drive to the Devereux building. After we had sex in the bathroom, Devon cleaned me up and then dressed.

True to his word, we found Liam in the kitchen, his eyes glued to his computer screen, going over the security footage, trying to figure out how the intruder got in and out without us knowing. He came to the conclusion that whoever the person was, they definitely had a key to the lock, and all the lock and alarm codes. They also knew exactly where each camera was. Things only the twins and Tate were aware of.

"I'll drop the two of you off, then go home and change the locks and codes," Liam tells us as we pull up in front of Devereux. "I'm also moving the cameras."

"Good idea," Devon tells his brother. "Pick us up before the city meeting. I want Rhyann there with us."

I get out of the car and walk over to the curb in front of the large building that houses all of Devereux Publications' companies. Liam steps out of the passenger seat and pulls the seat forward for Devon. Both brothers are nearly the same height, and stand almost a foot above me at six foot six. It's a little cruel to expect either one of them to sit in the back seat of such a small car when I'm small enough to sit back there with room to spare. But Donna is my baby and they know and respect that.

"You'll call me as soon as you confront Adrian?" Liam asks, pulling me into his arms.

"Of course," I assure him.

When I left his brother's room, I expected things to be awkward between us. There's no way he didn't know we had sex. But there was nothing but love and adoration in his eyes when he looked up from his computer. The same love and adoration reflected in his gaze as he looks down at me now, in public for all the world to see.

"Good girl." Liam winks at me before brushing his lips softly against my own. "Now, go slay the dragon and take over your company." He nods at his twin as the two of us leave him with Donna.

When Devon and I reach the thirty seventh floor, the floor that houses all the corporate offices for Devereux Publications, there's an excited buzz in the air that makes my hair stand up.

"What's going on?" Devon whispers as we step off the elevator.

"I'm not sure," I answer. "But Adrian's usually in one of the conference rooms around this time. He likes to meet with everyone first thing in the morning every Monday, and at the end of the day every Friday."

"Let's do this," Devon takes a deep breath and grips my hand. Together we make our way to the large conference room at the end of the hallway.

A few feet down the hall, we pass a few assistant desks. They're all occupied by young men and women. All college students looking for temp work in the field of business or publications. The only desk that's empty is the one I filled until today.

"Rhyann," Sarah, a young brunette, exclaims as we pass the bank of desks. "I heard you quit," she says, walking over to hug me. "I'm going to miss you."

I'm taken aback by her words. Why would anyone say I quit? I own the company, and the building. Awkwardly, I hug the girl back, looking around as the other assistants stare at us curiously.

"What makes you think she quit?" Devon asks, his own curiosity beating me to the punch.

"The obnoxious wanna-be queen bee blonde who came in with Mister Crawford's son this morning said so," a different assistant, a young man named Owen, answers from his desk.

"Aubree," I say under my breath.

"Oh, you know her?" Sarah asks.

"Unfortunately," Devon mumbles.

I don't hide the smile on my face. "Don't worry Sarah, I haven't quit. I own the company, remember?"

"Yeah." She nods and walks back to her desk. "I was just worried you were going to leave the company to be run by her and the Crawfords. That's the buzz around the office." When she shares that last bit of gossip, her voice is low, like she doesn't want anyone else to overhear her sharing it with me.

"She's actually here to squash all that today," Devon assures the group of assistants who have been the closest thing to friends I've had for the past four summers.

THE SECRETS THAT WE KEEP   291

"Has Mister Montgomery come in?" I ask Sarah quietly.

"He arrived just a couple minutes before you did. Mister Crawford is with him in his office now."

"Perfect. Tell no one I'm here, okay?" I smile at my little ragtag band of temps. "Sarah, will you have security on standby, just in case I need to have anyone removed from the building?"

She nods in understanding as Devon and I make our way to Adrian's office. My heart races as I think of all the possible outcomes of the meeting to come. Will Adrian make a scene? Will I have to have him escorted out? As my mind thinks of all the ways this could go south, I can't help but circle back to why Tate and Aubree would be here.

Devon squeezes my hand as we pause in front of the big glossy black doors of Adrian's office, my office. I look up at him and can see the same thoughts and worries reflected in his eyes. We both feel betrayed by someone who we've trusted with our lives since we were barely out of diapers.

With a deep breath, I push the doors open and step into a war zone. Boisterous men are talking over one another, each raising their voices to out-talk the other. Aubree sits daintily in a seat behind Adrian's, the seat I typically sit in during meetings with other members of Devereux, or with CEOs of other companies.

She's the first to notice our intrusion. "What are you doing here?" she snarls.

Ignoring her, I turn to Adrian, who's arguing with Calvin Montgomery—my lawyer— and clear my throat.

"Rhyann, what are you doing here? I thought with everything that happened over the weekend you were taking time off?" Adrian asks, feigning concern.

I ignore his question as well, a new sense of courage coursing through my veins. With a confidence I didn't know existed in me, I turn to Calvin. "Did you bring the paperwork I asked you to bring, Mister Montgomery?"

"I did." He nods.

"What's all this about?" the third man speaks up. I don't recognize him from any past meetings, but he carries an air of self importance that makes me want to slap him. "Crawford, who is this girl? Aubree, have someone call security."

"Yes, daddy," she says, and then rushes out of the office with an evil grin on her face.

"Shouldn't you be with my son?" Adrian looks at Devon. "Working on your little nightclub project?"

"Well, I was hired to protect Miss Devereux after," Devon smirks at Adrian, "everything that happened this weekend."

"Miss Devereux, hmm," Aubree's father muses. "Good, can you please clear up this absurd business with your lawyer so that Mister Crawford and I can get back to business?"

"And what business might that be?" I ask, settling into the big chair at Adrian's desk. The same desk my grandfather built this company from decades ago.

"That is none of your concern, child," the man cuts me off.

I can feel Devon's body vibrate with rage. I don't need to look up at him to know he is ready to tear the older man apart with his teeth. I place my palm against Devon's side, to calm myself as much as to calm him.

"I assure you, Mister—"

"Miller," he offers. I knew that. But he doesn't know that I know his daughter, at least I don't think he does. For all I know, he's in on whatever Tate and his father are planning.

"Mister Miller, as the CEO of Devereux Publications—" I start.

"Not yet, Rhyann." Adrian looks down at me, something in his expression I can't quite make out.

"Actually." I rest my elbows on the desk, my index fingers pointed as I rest my chin on them and smile up at Adrian. "I checked with Calvin here, and my grandfather's will stated that I'm eligible to take over the company as soon as I graduate college. So."

"Rhyann, don't do this,"Adrian pleads.

"Is this what you came here for?" Mister Miller glares at Calvin Montgomery, who has been standing behind me stoically since I took my seat at my grandfather's desk.

I take command of the room, like the CEO I'm supposed to be. "That is what he came for, do you have an issue with that Mister Miller?"

"Rhyann, please. Can we discuss this privately, another time?" Adrian asks me quietly.

"Of course." I smile at him. "However, it doesn't change anything, Adrian."

Aubree returns, all smiles, gloating at the prospect of putting me in my place, the building security guards right behind her. "I'm back, daddy." She points at me. "That's the trespasser," she says, looking at the security guards.

The two uniformed men look from me to Aubree and back to me. I can't help but laugh out loud over their

THE SECRETS THAT WE KEEP 295

confused looks. "I'm so sorry for the mix up," I tell the two men. "Can you please show Mister and Miss Miller the door?"

"Excuse me? Who do you think you are?" Aubree stalks toward me.

"Aubree, enough." Her father's stern voice echoes through the office. "Crawford, we will continue our discussion tonight."

"Daddy," Aubree whines from the door, both security guards now standing on each side of her.

"Aubree, you're fired," I tell her with a smile as her and her father leave the office.

Within minutes, it's just me, Adrian, Devon, and Calvin. The chaos and noise has died down to an uncomfortable silence. I look at the faces of each of the men in the room with me. Adrian stands by the window, eyes cast down. Calvin picks his nails, likely wishing he were anywhere but here at this moment. It's Devon's face I focus on. His eyes are full of pride and lit with encouragement. It's all I need to continue with what I came here to do.

"Why'd you lie to me, Adrian?" I ask, breaking the silence.

"I never lied, Rhyann," he sighs. "So much you don't even know about."

"Like your relationship with my grandfather?" I ask softly.

His head snaps in my direction, his eyes glossy. That got his attention. I didn't say it to out him, but to make a point. An important point that I have yet to get to. "You don't know what you're talking about."

"You're right, I don't. Is that why you had my grandfather's laptop stolen?" All three men in the room look at me. All three with different expressions on their faces. Adrian's is one of confusion and pain, Calvin looks concerned and a little out of place, and Devon still looks like he wants to strangle someone.

"What are you talking about, Rhyann?" Adrian asks me. The pain and sadness in his face wash away, leaving a concerned look.

"Last night's break in. The only thing they stole was my grandfather's laptop and all the files Calvin gave me." I glance at Calvin and watch as my words register in his mind.

"They stole the proof of your adoption?" he asks.

I nod my head slowly.

"Your house was broken into?" Adrian's head snaps to Devon. "You were supposed to set up a tight security system to prevent that."

"And we did. Someone knew how to bypass it." Devon's words are true, but the accusation behind them is obvious as well.

"Rhyann, where were you when it happened?"

I watch Adrian's demeanor change. Minutes ago, when I first mentioned my grandfather and the laptop, his shoulders and back were rigid, he looked crazed and defensive. Now, he's watching me protectively, like a father watches his baby girl.

"I was home," I tell him, looking down at my hands. "I was in the family room, about to watch a movie when I heard someone in my bedroom."

Adrian charges at Devon, gripping his shirt with his fist. I never realized how big of a man Adrian is until just now. He isn't as tall as Devon and Liam, but he does surpass the six foot mark, and the way he carries his fit frame reflects a man who is more than the suit he wears and the desk he sits behind.

"You had one job, and that was to keep her safe," he growls at Devon. "Do you know why I gave you that job?"

"Adrian, I am safe." I stand up like my five foot two self could do anything to separate these two giants of men.

"I asked you to do it because it's no secret how you feel about her." Adrian completely ignores me. "You love her more than you love your own twin, and you still failed to keep her safe."

"I. Am. Safe." I say a bit louder. This time, when they both ignore my presence, I put my hands between them and push, making room for me to stand and face the two men.

"Rhyann, please." Adrian looks down at me, his eyes filled with tears. "You're the closest thing I have to a daughter. Everything I've done since your grandfather died has been to protect you."

Devon remains stoic and silent, as though Adrian were speaking the thoughts he was too afraid to speak. I want to hold him, tell him how he has kept me safe, how he still keeps me safe, but something in the expression on his face tells me that he needs to have some space. "Dev, do you mind if I talk to Adrian alone?"

"Are you sure?" he asks me, finally looking me in the eyes.

"I'm sure. I don't think anything's going to happen to me while I'm with Adrian, do you?" My voice is soft,

THE SECRETS THAT WE KEEP   299

gentle, as though I'm talking to a frightened child. Or an
angry bear, in Devon's case.

"Fine." He bends down to kiss my temple. "Be careful
how much you tell him," Devon whispers in my ear before he stands up straight and turns to Calvin. "Let's go."

"Tell me about you and my grandfather, please," I ask
once Adrian and I are alone together.

"You know, I don't think he ever meant to keep anything from you," Adrian tells me as he pulls a chair up to
the front of the desk and sits down.

Rather than sit behind the large desk, I take the seat
beside Adrian and listen for at least an hour as he tells me
about how he accidentally fell in love with my grandfather. He loved his wife too, of course. He actually con-
sidered himself straight most of his life. He tells me that
he still does.

"There was just something incredible about your
grandfather that made me feel free, made me love myself
as much as I loved him," Adrian says with a sad, far
off look in his eyes. "Right before he died, he started
getting these strange emails from an unknown address.
The sender claimed to know you were adopted and they
threatened to expose you as a fraud."

"A fraud?" I ask. "A fraud for what?"

Adrian shrugs his shoulders. "Honestly, I don't know. They said you weren't the true heir." He laughs and shakes his head. "As though we are living in some fantastical story of kings and kingdoms and heirs."

This much I already knew. I had pieced it together from the emails that were left on my grandfather's computer. "Okay, so I'm still confused on how all this relates to me, the company, and everything that's happened in the past few days," I admit. "Why try to trick me into waiting until my birthday to take over the company?"

"Because I was hoping to save you from losing it." His explanation does almost nothing to comfort me. If anything, it sends me into a panic. My heart starts to race and my chest tightens, making it hard for me to breathe.

"Wha—What do you mean, lose the company?" I ask, trying not to show my fear.

"Before you were born, your grandfather had his will drawn up to say his son or grandchild would inherit his estate and Devereux Publications. It was supposed to be changed to your name, specifically, but he died before he could do that."

"Okay, and?" I can tell that Adrian's leaving something out. There's a secret he's keeping, something that is the key to this entire mess.

THE SECRETS THAT WE KEEP   301

"The person threatening to expose you was also claiming to be your father's biological son."

"Impossible. My mother couldn't have children."

Adrian looks away. "Your mother isn't his mother, Rhyann."

"So, are you saying I have a brother?" I have to ask. I have to know.

"Well, technically you don't. Even legally, Calvin says he doesn't have a leg to stand on. But with enough money and the right paperwork for proof, he could fight the will, block you from receiving your inheritance."

"And how do you know this person is telling the truth?"

Adrian turns back to look at me, tears falling from his long, dark lashes. "Because I was there when he was born. I helped his mother drop him off at the fire station."

His words feel like a punch to the gut. I'm dizzy, out of breath, and want to throw up all at the same time. "What do you mean, Adrian?"

"His mother is my ex-wife, Lenora. Tate's mother."

Chapter 26

Rhyann

After the bombshell of a revelation from Adrian, Devon and I told him and Calvin everything that happened last night. He explained that whoever is breaking into our homes has to be someone close. At least close enough to us that they're able to get copies of our keys and know our lives and schedules well.

Adrian looked as though someone shot him in the chest when he put the information together, forming the same thoughts the twins and I had this morning. I felt bad for him after everything. I told him that I wasn't sure if I was ready to take the company on by myself, and asked if he would help me ease into the position over the course of the next few months. He agreed, asked me to be his date for the gala tonight, and when I agreed, he sent me home.

THE SECRETS THAT WE KEEP   303

So now, Devon and I are shopping for dresses. I haven't been to a black tie event in ages, and I hadn't planned to attend one anytime soon. Especially the event where Adrian planned to announce his son's engagement to my biggest nightmare.

Yet here I am buying the fanciest red dress I've ever seen. One reason I hate these formal events is the floor length gowns the women are expected to wear. I'm barely above five feet tall, and those things make me look shorter than I already am. Thankfully, Devon finds me something more my style. Something the both of us can appreciate.

The dress is red, and it comes to my knees with a three inch slit up one side for better movement. It hugs all my curves and pushes my tits up like a corset would. It's one sleeved, and the sleeve goes all the way down to my wrist. It comes with a sheer black overcoat that molds to the body and flows down to the floor to make the dress black tie appropriate. I love it.

"I plan to watch as my brother fucks you in this tonight," Devon whispers from behind me as I look at myself in the mirror. I can see my cheeks turn as red as the dress. We haven't talked about what happened this morning in his bathroom, or the weird, maybe shared throuple we might have started.

"Devon." I smile at his reflection in the mirror.

"Don't try to get out of it, princess. There's no turning back, remember?"

I turn around to face him, not sure what I'm going to say. I just know I need to say something. "I—"

I'm cut off by the vibrating of his cellphone in his pants pocket. I take a breath of relief as he pulls the phone out and answers it. I know it's Liam based on the expression on Devon's face when he answers. We missed the city meeting today for The Dive, the speakeasy nightclub Tate founded with the twins.

I almost feel bad for missing the meeting, but after my encounter with Aubree first thing this morning, meeting with her and Tate on their turf was not my idea of a pleasant afternoon.

So, Devon sent his brother a text, telling him everything that happened since we separated and asked if his brother would just call him during the meeting. Now, Devon leaves me to get out of the dress and make my purchase. I'm a little surprised when he returns a few minutes later, ready to throat punch someone.

"I take it the meeting didn't go as you'd hoped?" I ask with a sympathetic smile.

"Depends on how you look at it." He offers me his hand as we walk down to the waiting Uber. "Aubree somehow managed to weasel her way in as a business partner. I am really starting to dislike this girl."

"Well, if it makes you feel any better, I hate her." I laugh.

"No? You don't say?" It's not often Devon lets his guard down enough to make a joke or be sarcastic. I love seeing this side of him though.

"We went to school together at Evangeline's. She was horrible back then. I'm not sure if she remembers me. But I didn't use Rhyann when I was there, I used my middle name."

"Sophia." Devon nods. It was my mother's name. Not my biological mother, but the one who raised me. It was my way of keeping her with me, keeping her spirit alive as I went to boarding school.

"Yeah," I sigh. "So what did Liam say?"

"He said he can't wait to see you in that dress."

Hours later, I'm standing at the top of a grand staircase inside some huge banquet hall. Devon is on one side of me, wearing a black on black satin tuxedo, and Liam is on the other. His tux is also black but he chose to go with deep crimson accents in an attempt to coordinate with me.

Kathleen happily drove over to the guys' apartment and helped with my hair. The entire time she was there, she told me all about how she would do my mother's hair whenever her and my dad would join my grandfather at events. I ended up with my hair in a messy bun at the top of my head, red curls and strings of shimmery black beads weaving in and out of the bun, spilling down in random places.

"I don't think I can do this." I look at the two men on either side of me.

"Of course you can, princess." Liam smiles down at me. His radiant grin brightens up the room, bathing me in its energy and warmth.

"We aren't leaving your side, I promise, Rhyann." Devon gives my arm a squeeze before we descend the stairs.

Tate never came home this afternoon. He told Liam he had to take care of Aubree after her traumatic experience at Devereux this morning. When Liam relayed the news

THE SECRETS THAT WE KEEP

to me and Devon, we both laughed hysterically before going into detail about how she left to get security, just to find out they came to escort her off the premises.

It still hurts too much to give Tate a lot of thought. The idea of him marrying someone like Aubree was painful enough, but to think that he has some part in whoever it is that's been stalking and torturing me over the past week, that feels like a knife to my heart. Tate has always been my protector, and to know he's been putting me in harm's way is almost too much to bear.

With a deep breath, I take the first step into the event. It's no surprise when conversations hush and eyes turn in our direction. The majority of the people here tonight are colleagues of Adrian's. They work in the multimedia industry in some capacity. There's a few faces I recognize from when my grandfather was still alive, people he rubbed elbows with. Those are the ones who give us polite smiles and friendly nods as we walk by.

The rest of the people in attendance must be acquaintances of Mister Miller, Aubree's father. The looks they give us makes me want to shrink inside myself. Their eyes are telling me I don't belong in this world, and their hushed whispers wondering what I'm doing here confirms my feelings.

"Rhyann," Adrian calls joyfully from across the room. He pushes through the crowd. "Boys, I'm glad all three of you could make it tonight."

"Wouldn't miss it for the world," Liam says, shaking Adrian's hand.

"Honestly, I would have expected an invitation sooner, sir," Devon says. "Being your son's best man and all."

"I'm sorry, son. I can't speak for Tate, but I'm sure with everything that's gone on the past week, it must have slipped his mind."

"Hmm." Devon nods, not wanting to rehash the pain from this morning.

"Rhyann, I was wondering if you'd be willing to join me on stage in a few minutes," Adrian addresses me, nodding in the direction of a small, brightly lit stage that's decorated with varying flower vases and small topiaries.

"Uh, sure," I say hesitantly. "I need a drink. And food."

"Of course." Adrian smiles at the three of us. "Boys, Rhyann, I'll come find you when it's time."

With a tight smile and short nod, Adrian returns to the circle of people he was talking to when we arrived. I've never been to one of these things, so I'm not sure if there's a buffet table and we just get in line for our food, or if there's actual wait staff that walk around taking orders or handing out hors d'oeuvres to everyone standing around.

"How do we get food here?" Liam asks.

"Hell if I know," his brother replies. "This is my first time coming to one of these."

"So, you're a virgin?" I snort. I have a habit of making bad jokes in awkward situations, and tonight is as awkward as it gets.

Devon laughs maniacally. "Princess, I promise you, there is nothing virginal about me."

"Nothing?" I question, glancing over at Liam with an arched brow.

Liam just shrugs his shoulders and smiles as we weave through the throng of people looking for two things. One, food. Two, a quiet place to sit and wait.

We find the sets of round tables at the far end of the banquet hall. Most tables are empty. A few have some of the older guests sitting at them, the people who have been to one too many charity events and couldn't care less about the gossip circles anymore.

The guys and I occupy the table closest to the emergency exit. Devon reasons that it'll be easier to sneak out if there's a scene, or any kind of trouble with Tate and

Aubree tonight. After this morning's debacle, he says he doesn't trust either of them.

It still hurts when I think about Tate and how he's turned his back on me in such an epic way. I worry about what he'll do when he realizes what's going on between me and Devon. Well, me, Devon, and Liam. I don't know what we are, or if we are anything. I just know that after this morning, they're both mine, and I'm theirs.

"I'm gonna go find out how we go about getting dinner here. Isn't it like five hundred dollars a plate or something?" Liam asks after I settle in at the table.

I watch Liam walk away, his tuxedo making him blend into the crowd. He and Devon grew up in much the same way as Tate and I. They never needed or wanted for anything in life. Their parents had great careers and were able to provide for them well. The difference in all of us was the home dynamic.

The Morris family put each other above social status, or money, or any of the mortal trappings that so many in attendance tonight value. You'd never catch Mister and Missus Morris at an event like this, whereas my grandfather and Adrian flourish in this world.

Devon doesn't say anything after he sits down beside me. He's busy on his phone. I look over, my curiosity

THE SECRETS THAT WE KEEP   311

getting the better of me, and catch a snippet of a conversation between him and Tate.

Tate: Why is she here with you guys?

Devon: She's my date. She used to be your best friend too, remember

Tate: Whatever, she better behave, or it's on you.

Devon: Roger, boss

What the hell? I don't know what to say or what to even think about what I'm reading over his shoulder. When he sees me looking in his direction, he closes his phone and puts it in his pocket quickly.

Panic begins to wash over me as I imagine the conversation before what I just read. Did I put my trust in the wrong people? What if this is all an elaborate head game that all three of them concocted? Oh god, I'm going to be sick.

"Are you okay, princess?" Devon asks, resting his big hand between my shoulder blades.

"Yeah." I clear my throat. "I think I just need to use the restroom."

"Let's go then," Devon says, standing from his seat.

"No, you stay here," I tell him. What I really need is a minute away from him. "What if someone takes our table or Liam brings food back?"

"I don't like the idea of you going off alone, Rhyann."
Devon sighs.

My heart aches hearing the longing in the way he says
my name. I want to trust him, I want to believe that he
meant every word he said to me this morning. But, what
did he really say to me? That I belong to him, and I always
have? Well, I belonged to him when I was sixteen and he
broke my heart. Someone can want to possess a person
but not love them.

"I'll be fine, Devon. Promise." I point to the hall not
too far from where we sit, and the black sign that has the
word "Restroom" written in white letters. "See, you can
watch me from here. What can possibly happen?"

"Fine, but if you take too long, I'll come in there and
get you myself." He sits back down and folds his thick
arms over his chest.

"Promises, promises." I force a smile as I walk in the
direction of that hallway.

There's a breeze in the hallway once I get past the area
visible to the dining room. It's longer than I expected,
and after a few feet, the wall blocks my view of the dining
area and the rest of the banquet hall. I pass the men's
room and turn right when the hallway turns. On my
left is the door to the ladies' room, and in front of me

THE SECRETS THAT WE KEEP

is another emergency exit door. It's propped open by something on the floor, and that must be the source of the breeze.

Knowing the week I've had, I know it'd be a bad idea to let my curiosity get the better of me. Something settles in the pit of my stomach and I decide I'd rather take my chances with the two men I know I can't trust, rather than trying my luck with the unknown. I turn around to walk back to my table when I smack into a tall, lanky body.

I stumble back, but before I can see who's in front of me, a rag is placed over my mouth. There's a pungently sweet odor coming from the cloth and right away my head starts to swim.

"Hello, Ginger. I told you I'd see you soon," is all I hear before everything goes black.

To be continued...

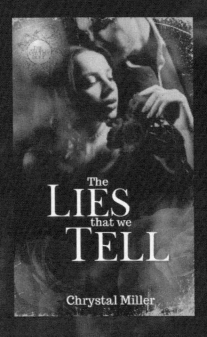

February 2024

About the Author

Chrystal is a proud Californian who loves to read and write. She has had many life experiences that she channels into her writing.
She has the support of a loving husband who willingly accompanies her on her many adventures.
She is the mother to three incredible children, as well as a fur mom to a crazy pug, four cats, and a bunny.
Chrystal is a nature and animal lover. When she's not reading or writing, one of her favorite things to do is to take the roads less traveled and find the magical places in nature.

Thank you

Caleb, my husband, the love of my life and my light in the darkness. Where would I be without you? Where would this book, the ones before it, and the ones that will come next be without your love and unwavering support? Thank you for being there, encouraging me to push through the hard days and revel in the happy ones. Its because of you that I'm able to follow my dreams.

Jon, Selene, and Gunner, my babies (even though I know you're not babies anymore) I hope my example for you is one worthy of following. I love you all more than you'll ever know.

Nikki, my author bestie. Thank you for keeping me focused and reminding me of the finish line.

Danny and Ashley, my editors. Thank you for all the hard work you've put into seeing this book make it to the pages.

Also By Chrystal Miller

Coming Soon

FEBRUARY 2024

OCTOBER 2023

STALK ME

Made in the USA
Las Vegas, NV
17 October 2023